A HARLEM MOON
CLASSIC

TAMBOURINES TO GLORY

*

A Novel

LANGSTON HUGHES

HARLEM MOON

Broadway Books

New York

PUBLISHED BY HARLEM MOON

Copyright © 1958 by Langston Hughes. Copyright renewed 1986 by George Houston Bass.

All Rights Reserved

A previous edition of this book was originally published in 1958 by The John Day Company. It is here reprinted by arrangement with the Estate of Langston Hughes.

Published in the United States by Harlem Moon, an imprint of The Doubleday Broadway Publishing Group, a division of Random House, Inc., New York.
www.harlemmoon.com

Reading Group Companion by La Marr J. Bruce.

HARLEM MOON, BROADWAY BOOKS, and the HARLEM MOON logo, depicting a moon and a woman, are trademarks of Random House, Inc. The figure in the Harlem Moon logo is inspired by a graphic design by Aaron Douglas (1899–1979).

The author and publisher gratefully acknowledge the following for the right to reprint material in this book:
"Precious Lord, Take My Hand," words and music by Thomas A. Dorsey, © 1938 Unichappell Music, Inc. Copyright renewed. Rights for the extended term of copyright in the U.S. assigned to Warner-Tamerlane Publishing Corp. All rights reserved. Used by permission of Alfred Publishing Co., Inc.

Library of Congress Cataloging-in-Publication Data
Hughes, Langston, 1902–1967.
    Tambourines to glory : a novel / Langston Hughes.— 1st Harlem Moon trade pbk. ed.
       p. cm. — (Harlem Moon classic)
     1. African American women—Fiction. 2. Churches—Fiction.
3.   Gospel music—Fiction. 4. Good and evil—Fiction. 5. Harlem (New York, N.Y.)—Fiction. I. Title. II. Series.

PS3515.U274T3 2006
813'.52—dc22

2006041113

ISBN-13: 978-0-7679-2327-9
ISBN-10: 0-7679-2327-8

PRINTED IN THE UNITED STATES OF AMERICA

10 9 8 7 6 5 4 3 2 1

First Edition

Contents

Introduction

Tambourines to Glory is an old-fashioned but modernized moral-ity play or tale based in Harlem where good and evil tussle over souls. At the core is the tug-of-war between the "likker"-drenched hustler Laura Wright Reed and the stolid, God-fearing Essie Belle Johnson. Though both trace their roots to somewhere in the South, they represent the clash of urban slickness with backwoods purity and simplicity. Both have had their share of "no-good men."

It's Laura's scheme for the two women to get some tam-bourines and become street-corner evangelists in order to raise money to pay the rent, to buy "likker," and to get rich quick. That Langston Hughes chose to focus on gospel and storefront churches probably stemmed from what he saw happening around him in Harlem in the late 1950s.

While the civil rights movement was beginning to flex its muscles in the South, Harlem was still caught in the throes of an unrelenting slump where unemployment, dilapidated buildings, rampant racism, and police brutality combined to nullify hope and progress among most of the community's destitute residents. The real-life counterparts of Laura and Essie didn't experience the avenues of opportunity until the careers of New York political leaders like Hulan Jack and J. Raymond Jones fully blossomed in the 1960s. This was also a time when many singers were crossing over from gospel to rhythm and blues or rock and roll. Hughes makes several references to this trend in the novel.

Laura and Essie are so successful at preaching that they soon are no longer on the street corner but are the proud proprietors of a run-down theater that they renovate into their church. As they prosper, the size of their congregation increases, attracting an assortment of misfits, including Big-Eyed Buddy Lomax, who seduces Laura (or does she seduce him?).

Tambourines to Glory, first published in 1958, was Hughes's second novel, though unlike his *Not Without Laughter* (1930), it is rarely mentioned. This oversight may stem from the fact that *Not Without Laughter* was written first and almost a generation before *Tambourines to Glory*; thus, it would appear on more lists and bibliographies than the later published novel. In addition, it's possible that many readers and critics perceive *Tambourines* more as a play than a novel.

"Did I tell you I've just finished a little novel called *Tambourines to Glory* about the goings-on in gospel churches?" Hughes wrote in a letter to his friend Carl Van Vechten. "Also made a play of it with a Tambourine Chorus and two women preacher-songsters, one sweet, one naughty . . ."

This letter from Hughes to one of his literary mentors was written in September 1956. However, we know from Arnold Rampersad, in his two-volume study of Hughes's life, that there was earlier correspondence between Hughes and his lifelong friend and collaborator Arna Bontemps about *Tambourines to Glory* suggesting the play preceded the novel.

According to Rampersad, Hughes began working on the "drama" on July 14, 1956, and finished it in ten days. It was entitled *Tambourines to Glory: A Play with Songs*. In his letter to Bontemps he exclaimed: "It's a singing, shouting, wailing, drama of the old conflict between blatant Evil and quiet Good, with the Devil driving a Cadillac."

(It should be noted that there are several places in the novel where stage directions appear to be vestiges of the play. Or, Hughes may have deliberately added them to set the scenes in a stylized way.)

Whether the novel preceded the play or vice versa may be a moot point since there is no dramatic difference between them. There is a difference, though, in the time in which they reached the public. The novel was published in 1958, while the play, after enduring a troubled and delayed arrival, did not appear on Broadway until 1963, lasting only twenty-five performances. Most of the reviews lambasted the play, citing it as "slapped together" and containing a "shifting point of view."

On the other hand, reviews of the novel were comparatively generous. "As a literary work," wrote Gilbert Millstein of the *New York Times*, "*Tambourines to Glory* is skillful and engaging—the consistently high quality of Hughes's production over the years is, considering its great quantity, a remarkable phenome- non and the mark of an exuberant professionalism."

If, in essence, the play and the novel are the same, why would one be so woefully dismissed and the other praised? It might be the portrayals of the characters, the perception of the critics, or, as I propose, the play's inability to capture all the humor, irony, subtleties, nuances, figures of speech, folklore, and cultural refer- ences that enliven the novel. Not only does Hughes develop com- pelling characters—and more than one literary critic has noted the similarities between the protagonists, Laura Reed and Essie, and Zarita and Joyce from the "Simple" tales—he gives them set- tings and contexts in which to express colorful language, and in which Hughes can show vital musical correlations.

Thinking about the play, I don't recall the wealth of verbal ex- changes between Laura and Essie that abound in the novel, the sharp contrasts they draw between the black urban and rural experiences. Nor is it possible to capture in the play format Hughes's omniscient narrator, who repeatedly invokes jazz metaphors, likening the tambourine players' beat to the drums of Cozy Cole, or Eve's complexion in a Garden of Eden mural to that of Sarah Vaughan.

The novel allows readers to create their own images of the characters, and Hughes was a master at sparking a reader's imag- ination, teasing us with hilarious concoctions, clever sayings, and memorable folks. Many of us know somebody like Birdie Lee, Big-Eyed Buddy Lomax, and Chicken Crow-For-Day. But, above all, there is the simple, lyrical quality of Hughes's writing that never strains the reader's credulity, to paraphrase the late Darwin Turner.

There is no need here to overwhelm you with some of the more interesting turns in the plot or the redemptive surprises; I leave those for you to laugh at and to mull over. Just as *Tambourines to Glory* the play has been variously revived, now its predecessor— or successor, depending on the source—is being reissued. And it may be in the theater of your mind that this Hughes creation is best realized.

HERB BOYD

HARLEM

DECEMBER 15, 2005

TAMBOURINES TO GLORY

To Irene

Upon this Rock I build my
Church and the gates of hell
shall not prevail against it.

PALM SUNDAY

It was a chilly Palm Sunday and Essie Belle Johnson did not have a palm. Several of the other kitchenette dwellers in her lodgings had been to church that day and returned with leaves, sheaves and even large sprays of palm straw to stick up in their mirrors or in one corner of the frame of Mama's picture.

"I used to always go to church on Palm Sunday when I were a child," Essie said, "as well as Easter, too."

"I seldom went," said Laura, "and never regular. My mother was too beat out from Saturday night to get me up in time to go to church. My step-pa sold whiskey—you know, I growed up in boot-leg days. My schooling came from bathtub likker, with some small change left over sometimes to go to movies, buy Eskimo pies."

"My mama always woke me up on the Sabbath before she went

to work," mused Essie. "Her white folks only gave her one Sunday off a month. She'd give me a nickel to put in Sunday school and a dime for church, then leave something in the pot for me to eat when I got back home. In the evening, Mama would go to services by herself and turn out the light and leave me in bed until I got teen-age. Then I went to church at night, too. I loved those songs, 'Precious Lord, Take My Hand.' Oh, but that's pretty! Let's go to church Easter, Laura."

"Which one, Sanctified or Baptist?"

"Where the singing is best," said Essie.

"Sanctified," said Laura. "But you know I ain't got nothing to wear to church. On Easter Sunday I should decorate my headlights proper. Man told me last week, said, 'Woman, you got bubbies like the headlights on a Packard car sticking out like two forty-fours. Stop shooting me in the eyes that way with what you carries in front of you.'" Laura drew herself up proudly.

"An out-of-shape woman can get by with some poor rags. But you got a good figure, Laura. If you didn't put so much money into the bottle, you could get yourself some clothes."

"Girl, hush! Chilly as it is tonight, I had to get a little wine. Being Sunday, I had to pay more for it bootleg. There ought to be some heat in this old rat-hole."

"You could have got yourself a hat with what you paid for that wine."

"*An Easter bonnet with a blue ribbon on it,*" sang Laura. "Pshaw, child, by this time next Sunday I might have a new hat. Who knows? Maybe my new man will buy me one."

"If he does, it will be mighty near the first time. You one of these women always buying men something, instead of letting them do for you. You sure are crazy about men, Laura."

"One nice thing about being on relief is, it leaves you plenty time to be sweet to your daddy, have him something ready to eat when he comes from work, have your own head combed. I don't see much sense in a woman working, long as the Home Relief mails out checks. Of course, sometimes I has more energy being idle than I know what to do with. Essie, if I could just set on my haunches and be content like you! You don't even want a drink— just set and get fat, and you're happy."

"I ain't all that happy, Laura. I want my daughter with me. I get lonesome. If it wasn't for you dropping in all the time, I'd be more lonesome. Sure glad you're my neighbor, Laura, even if I can't keep you company with no bottle."

"A few swallows of this and you'd forget about being lonesome. You ought to learn to drink a little, Essie."

"I hate that old raw wine, Laura. It makes me sick at the stomach."

"Your life is empty and your belly, too. You ought to do something. At least, get yourself a man, girl, somebody, anybody."

"A man?" cried Essie. "No! Not to beat me all over the head. I'm cranky. I'm getting set in my ways. And I been long disgusted with men, low-down, no-good as they are."

"Well, smoke a reefer then. Try a little goopher dust. Dope, nope? Live out your life, instead of just setting here gathering pounds. Excite yourself, get high and fly."

"Somehow I kinder like to keep my head clear. Even if I am beat, I like to know it."

"Woman, you sound right simple," declared Laura.

"Anyhow, where would I get the money for them bad habits you're talking about, even if I wanted them?"

"The Lord helps them that helps themselves," declared Laura, shaking the last drop of sherry out of her pint bottle and laying it flat on the porcelain table. "Essie, don't you want no kind of pleasure out of living? You ain't that old. You still got breasts, legs, and what God give you. No fun, you might as well die."

"Sometimes I think so, rooming all by myself like this and living off the Welfare. About all I can do nowadays is ask the Lord to take my hand."

"Well, why don't you do that then? Get holy, sanctify yourself. The Lord is no respecter of persons if He takes a pimp's hand and makes a bishop out of him, like he did with Bishop Longjohn over there on Lenox Avenue. That saint had three whores on the block ten years ago. He's got a better racket now, the Gospel! And a rock and roll band out of this world in front of the pulpit with a piano player that beats Teddy Wilson. That bishop's found himself a great shill."

"Shill?"

"Racket, girl, racket."

"Religion don't just have to be a racket, Laura, do it? Maybe he's converted."

"Converted about as much as an atom bomb is converted to peace."

"Longjohn might be converted, Laura."

"All the money he takes in every Sunday would convert me," declared Laura. "Money! I sure wish I had some. Say, Essie, why don't you and me start a church like Mother Bradley's? We ain't doing nothing else useful, and it would beat Home Relief. You sing good. I'll preach. We'll both take up collection and split it."

"What denomination we gonna be?" asked Essie, amused at the idea.

"Start our own denomination, then we won't be beholding to nobody else," said Laura.

"Where we gonna start it?" asked Essie.

"Summer's coming, ain't it? We'll start it on the street where the bishop started his, right outdoors this summer, rent free, on the corner."

Essie grinned. "You mean, in the gutter where we are."

"On the curb above the gutter, girl. We'll save them lower down than us."

"Now, who could they be?"

"The ones who can do what you can't do, drink without getting sick, stay high on Sneaky Pete wine. Gamble away their rent. Play up their relief check on the numbers. Lay with each other without getting disgusted, no matter how many unwanted kids they produce. Use the needle, support the dope trade. Them's the ones we'll set out to convert."

"With what?"

"With Jesus. He comes free," cried Laura. "Girl, you know I think I hit upon an idea. Just ask Jesus to take your hand, in public, Essie. Then, next thing you know, somebody will think He's got your hand, and will put some cash in *yours* to see if they can make the same contact. Folks is simple. Money they're going to throw away anyhow, so they might as well throw some our way. Just walk with God, and tell the rest of them to follow you, *and pay as they go.* Dig?"

Taking it like an impossible game, Essie murmured, "Um-hum!" But Laura already saw herself as a lady preacher. Besides, the wine was gone. In her new role, she felt like singing, and she did.

"Precious Lord, take my hand,
Lead me on, let me stand.
I am weak, I am tired, I am worn."

She had a strange voice, deep, strong, wine-rusty, and wild.

"Through the storms of the night
Lead me on to the light.
Take my hand, precious Lord, lead me on."

Essie was moved. "I knowed you could sing blues, Laura, but I never knowed you knew them kind of songs before."

"Pick it up with me," said Laura. "Pick it up, girl."

Cooler, higher and sweeter than Laura's, Essie's voice picked up the song, and the drab cold kitchenette room filled with melody was no longer cold, no longer drab. Even the light seemed brighter.

"When my way grows drear,
Precious Lord, linger near.
When the day is almost gone,
Hear my cry, hear my call,
Guide my feet lest I fall.
Take my hand, precious Lord, lead me on."

"Essie, if I could sing like you, I'd be Mahalia Jackson," cried Laura. "You're a songster!"

"Mahalia is a good woman. I ain't," said Essie.

"To make her money, records and all, I'd be willing to be good myself," said Laura.

"It ain't easy to get hold of money. I've tried, Lord knows I've tried to get ahead. Ever since I come up North I been scuffling to get enough money to send for my daughter and get a little two-, three-room apartment for her and me to stay in."

"Pshaw! For love nor money can't nobody get no apartment in Harlem, unless you got enough money to pay under the table."

"Marietta's sixteen and ain't been with me, her mama, not two years hand-running since she were born. I always wanted that child with me. Never had her. Laura, I was borned to bad luck."

"Essie, it's because you don't use your talents, that's why," said Laura, looking at her portly friend with a critical eye. "All you use, like most women, is the what-you-may-call-it that you sets on, your assets instead of your head. Now, me, I got a brain, but I pay it no mind. I hope you will, though, and listen to my advice. Girl, with your voice, raise your fat disgusted self up out of that relief chair and let's we go make our fortune saving souls.

"Remember Elder Becton? Remember that white woman back in depression days, Aimee Semple McPherson, what put herself on some wings and opened up a temple and made a million dollars? Girl, we'll call ourselves sisters, use my name, the Reed Sisters. Even if we ain't no relation, we're sisters in God. You sing, I'll preach. We'll stand on the curb and let the sinners in the gutter come to us. You know, my grandpa down in North Carolina was a jackleg preacher. And when I get full of wine, I can whoop and holler real good. Listen to this spiel."

Laura jumped up from her chair with gestures. "I'll tell them Lenox Avenue sinners," she said, "you-all better come to Jesus! Yes, sinning like hell every night, you better, because the atom bomb's about to destroy this world, and you ain't ready! Get ready! Get ready! I say, aw, let Him take your hand. Yes, sisters, brothers, He's got mine! Let Him take yours and walk with Him. Now, sing with me:

> "When the darkness appears,
> Precious Lord, linger near.
> When my life is almost gone,
> At the river I stand,
> Guide my feet, hold my hand.
> Take my hand, precious Lord, lead me on.

"Grab the chorus, Essie. Sing it, girl, sing!"

Essie's voice rose full and persuasive, so persuasive, in fact, that melodically she persuaded herself and Laura, too, that they ought to go out into the streets and move multitudes.

"I sure wish I had me some more wine," sighed Laura when they had finished singing.

"The Wine of God is all we need," Essie said. "Laura, I'm gonna pray." She knelt down with her arms on the chair where she had been sitting. "Lord, I wish you would take my hand. Lead me on, show me the way, help me to be good. Help Sister Laura, too. And help us both to help others to be good. That I wish in my heart, Lord, I do."

"Amen!" cried Laura with her hand on her empty glass.

" 'Surely goodness and mercy shall follow me all the days of my life,' " murmured Essie.

"And never catch up with you unless you get up and do something yourself," said Laura.

2

BLUE MONDAY

The next morning, which was a blue Monday, when Laura could hardly scrape together enough change to combinate a number and put a dime on the lead, Essie said as she washed the percolator top, "I prayed again this morning for what we was talking about last night."

Laura, who had left her bed unmade down the hall in Number 7 to tap on Essie's door in the hope of a hot cup of coffee, looked puzzled. "What?"

"That church we gonna start," said Essie. "I believe God answers prayer. In fact, that church is started."

"Started? Where?"

"Right here in this room with you and me."

"Then lemme pass the collection plate," said Laura, "because

I dreamed about fish last night—782—and that is a good number to play. Here, put some change in this saucer, and I'll put the number in for you, too."

"I said I was *praying*, Laura, not playing. If we're gonna save souls, have I got to save you from sin first?"

"Oh, you talking about starting a church?" said Laura, her mind clearing of sleep a little. "Well, as soon as the weather warms up a bit, we'll buy a Bible and a tambourine and plant our feet on the rock of 126th and Lenox and start. But right now, I want me at least forty-five cents to work on these numbers. Suppose *fish* jumps out today? If it did, and I didn't catch it, I sure would be mad. Girl, pour me one little drop more of that coffee. If I could just find that old Negro who's liking me so much, so he says, I might could maybe get a dollar or two. But he never does come by here on Monday."

"Laura, you oughtn't to be encouraging that married man to be laying up with you."

"He encourages his self," yawned Laura. "Can I help it if I appeal to him whenever he can get out of his wife's sight? The Lord give me my smooth brown body, girl, and I ain't one to let it go to waste. Excuse me, I'm gonna comb my hair and go downstairs and put these numbers in. A small hit's better than none. But I sure hate to be so poor! Maybe that Chinese that winked at me from behind the lunch counter will feel in a lending mood this morning."

"A Christian woman taking up with a heathen," said Essie.

"On a blue Monday morning I would take up with a dog," said Laura, "if the dog said, 'Baby, how about a drink?' Soon as this coffee dies down, I'm gonna need something a little stronger."

Laura's carpet slippers heel-flapped their way down the hall. All the nearby kitchenettes were quiet. Everybody on that floor except these two women had gone to work. Essie sat down to think, and sat a long while, which was what she liked to do—just sit. Ten o'clock, eleven o'clock, noon. But today, she kept seeing in her mind's eye herself singing to more and more people on a corner, then in a gospel tent, then in a church, and people weeping and shouting and fainting and coming to Jesus because of her songs, and a railroad ticket, yellow and very long, that she was folding and putting into a letter and sending to her daughter in Richmond writing, "Honey, baby, daughter, child, come to your mother," and she was signing the letter with her own name, *Essie.* And suddenly she was shouting all alone by herself, "Thank you, God! Thank God! Thank God!"

Then she got up and started sweeping the floor, and imagined it was the living room of a nice apartment, and she was getting ready for Marietta to arrive. She looked out her rear window three stories down into a courtyard full of beer cans and sacks of garbage and saw, instead, a pretty view of a park—because where she lived now with her daughter was way up on the hill and there were trees outside the apartment windows. "It's all because of You, Lord," she said, "and because I am walking with God. Yes!" And she began to sing:

> *"Just a closer walk with Thee,*
> *Grant it, Jesus, if you please.*
> *Daily walking close to Thee—*
> *Let it be! Let it be! Let it be!"*

Broom in hand, she stopped. "I wonder if that wine-head of a Laura has sure enough converted me? Thank God, I see some kind of light right now!

"I am weak, but Thou art strong.
Jesus, keep me from all wrong!
I'll be satisfied as long
As I walk close to Thee!"

"Sing it, girl," cried Laura, breezing past in the hall to find the Chinese counterman in the Japanese restaurant, her numbers writer, and somebody on the corner to buy her a bottle of wine.

Essie sat down again in her chair, filling it amply, and again her mind was sort of empty as it usually was. But the sun came in bright at the window, brighter than the sun had been for many months. It was spring. Vaguely Essie thought, I'll raise the window in a minute. But she sat a long, long time before she did raise the window. Essie's life had been full of long, long, very long pauses.

3

VISIONS OF A ROCK

"Well, it did not hit," said Laura, "no parts of it. The number was 413—so I did not catch the lead, I did not catch the second, and I had no change to put on the third. That Chinese man did not feel so well today. What did you do all afternoon?"

Essie had a report to make. "I priced a Bible."

"Have I done dreamed up something that you are really taking serious," said Laura, "about this church?"

"Been passing the store for months and just never noticed," said Essie, "that stuck back up there in the window of that furniture household shop, midst stoves, hassocks, floor lamps, and overstuffed chairs, is a great big Bible leaning up against a sign that says: GOLD-EDGED BIBLE ON INSTALLMENT PLAN—*Two*

Dollars Down, Two Dollars a Month. That Bible costs eighteen-fifty."

"Where's it at?" asked Laura.

"Bernstein's," said Essie. "Big beautiful gold-lettered Bible. We might as well buy a big Bible."

"I agree," said Laura. "If I hit tomorrow, I'll put down the first payment."

"No," said Essie. "Let's start this thing right. When my Welfare check comes, I'll put down a payment. But let's not use no numbers money to found our church."

"You are getting holier-than-thou already," said Laura. "Girl, I believe I'll go take a little nap before nightfall. Old daddy-boy-baby might come by to keep me awake after dark. Dig you remotely, doll. So long!"

Concerning Laura, "She's got a fine brown frame," observed the men in the block. "A hefty hussy," said the women, "more well-built than plump, but there's enough of her." From behind, young boys might whistle, "Whee-ooo-oo-o!" But if Laura turned around they saw she could be their mother, but a good-looking mother for true. When Laura got dressed up, her exterior decorations hung well. Sometimes emerging from the Rabbit Warren with her finery on, Laura looked good. Well ahead of her came her breasts, natural—like singers' voices in the pre-microphone days, projecting without artificial aid—colloquially termed by the local Lotharios *headlights, forty-fours, easy riders, daily doubles, Maes,* meaning West. Concerning her legs, climbing stairs had kept them sturdy, dancing kept them graceful, pride kept them in runless stockings chosen to match her cocoa skin. Laura would buy stockings when she couldn't pay her rent. If a man said something nice about her legs on the subway, she would pull her dress down. Otherwise when seated she was careless. Guile, not modesty, generally prevailed.

Concerning the ancient building where Laura and Essie lived, well, if you didn't see all those names under the different bells, you wouldn't believe so many people lived there: B. Jenkins, Sarah Butler, J. T. K. Washington, Ben Wade, Mrs. E. B. Johnson (which was Essie), Katie Huff, Jefferson Lord, Jr., Mr. and Mrs. Titter, Sisseretta Smith, Ed Givens, Laura Wright Reed (which was Laura), and so on and on into the dozens and dozens, sometimes three or four people listed in the same room. It was an old apartment house in which a door opening onto the central hall had been cut directly into every room, and inner communicating doors sealed. Then each room no matter how small had been made into a kitchenette with a gas burner (fire laws notwithstanding) plus a sink installed in a corner for washing both face and feet, pots and privates, clothes, cutlery, dogs and dishes. The building had a name, the Marquette, but the neighborhood called it the *Rabbit Warren*, for short just the *Rabbit*.

Late that afternoon in the Rabbit, through the still-open window facing the areaway, Essie could hear kids coming home from school, romping and playing on other floors in rooms where parents had not yet come home from work. Alone, youngsters could make as much noise as they wished. Sometimes they made plenty. Essie did not mind. She kept thinking of her own child as still a little playful girl—only her daughter *couldn't* be like that any more. Marietta was sixteen. Essie had not seen her for four years, but Grandma had sent her a picture when the girl came out of junior high school, a golden-faced kid, all in white looking mighty pretty. Grandma kept that child looking washed and clean all the time.

She must be a church girl, thought Essie, because them people are religious down South. Well, when Marietta gets here, she will find me religious, too. Never was much of a sinner, nohow. I can't go for sin like Laura. Fast life tires me out.

Essie got up to pull down the window, since the sunset was chilly. She put on her coat, a shapeless, heavy old black coat, and sat down again. From the pocket of her coat she took a long pearl-handled knife, pressed a little button in its side and a thin sharp blade shot out. With the blade she began to clean her fingernails—which was about the only use she had ever had for that knife, although Essie carried it in her pocket when she went out, for protection, she said, against robberies and rapes and suchlike calamities. But nobody had ever even tried to snatch Essie's pocketbook, let alone otherwise accost her rather corpulent person.

Once in a while a man leaning on a stoop might say, "Big mama, you look good to me." But none had as yet tried to drag her into a hallway to rob her of her virtue, or pull her down a janitor's steps into a furnace room—where she had heard tell many a good woman had surrendered to males unknown. Had any man laid hands on her, "I have my knife," said Essie, as she used it to clean her fingernails.

When Essie had finished, she clicked the blade back in place, put her protector in her coat pocket, and sat for a long spell in the gathering dusk before she got up to turn on the light, wash the rice, and start to cook herself some supper. Might be maybe Laura would add something to the pot, and they would eat together. It was rather early in the week for Laura's Old Man to be coming by.

I need some rock on which to stand, suddenly thought Essie leaning over the stove. That Laura's got several rocks of an earthly nature on which she leans, men, numbers, likker, even if they do slip out from under her sometimes. While me, I just set, and set, and set. "But now I see me a rock, and that rock is Jesus!" cried Essie aloud.

Suddenly she was startled that her thoughts had become words rocking about the room, words spoken so strongly and with so much conviction that she almost dropped the spoon with which she stirred the rice.

Then much more quietly and quite aware of the fact that she was *talking,* not merely thinking, "A Rock," she cried, "I visions me a Rock."

4

NATURALLY WEAK

"Old raccoon, you," cried Laura, "if you can't bring me nothing, then don't come by here." Essie heard her friend's voice all the way up the hall. "Just stay home, Negro!"

"So you want me to stay home, huh?" growled the man.

His walking papers, Essie thought. But they don't have to let the world know every time they fall out. Some people are too broadcast.

"I can't come handing you out money every time I look in your face," barked the old raccoon.

"I know somebody who can," cried Laura. "And he's a young man, too."

Laura's lying, thought Essie. Laura gives that young man money herself every time her Welfare check comes. Uly do not give her a thing but a hard row to go. Laura is just trying to collect from that old man to *keep* that young man on her string. That Laura, mused Essie as she cut a great big piece of Cushman's cake to go with her third cup of tea. Laura's hungry, that I know, and since that old man did not bring no change with him, this being Monday, I know she just wants to get rid of him quick so she can come on in here and eat. Payday, he'll be welcome back.

> *I need some rock on which to stand,*
> *Some ground that is not shifting sand . . .*

Somehow the song kept running through her mind that she had heard so often on a gospel program over the radio from Jersey City. Everywhere, Jersey City, Richmond, New York, everywhere she had ever been, everybody needed some rock on which to stand. Essie found herself eating and singing. The song was beautiful and cool in the room when Laura tapped lightly and tripped on in. Laura said, "Well, all right, now!" and joined in the song until her food got warmed up. Meanwhile some of the other tenement dwellers opened up their doors to listen since it sounded as if there might be a small revival meeting going on in the room, and Essie heard somebody say, "That singing sure sounds good!"

Laura said, "You see, girl, I'm telling you, this religious jive is something we can collect on. Look here, ain't you got no meat or nothing to go with this rice jive here? I been wrastling with that old raccoon for the last two hours, I'm hungry. Maybe Uly will be by about ten or eleven o'clock—my heart, my lover-man for true! Ain't we got a ham hock left from Sunday I can put on my plate?"

"Your memory is short," said Essie. "You know we cleaned up

that ham hock and greens yesterday. Saturday, Sunday—how long you expect one pot of victuals to last?"

"The relief investigator thinks one pot ought to last a week. I sure will be glad when we ain't no longer beholding to them people. My investigator is colored, too—talking about she don't see why I can't get along on the money I draw. Also, as healthy-looking as I am, why can't I keep a job? And me, I done stooped myself over, uncombed my hair, tottered, and tried to look as sick and consumptive as I could for her benefit. We're both of the *same* race, she and me. Why does she begrudge me them white folks' money? Essie, you could at least have made some gravy for this rice. Even if I am from Carolina where it grows, I like a meat-flavor with rice, girl. I like meat! If 782 had just come out, we could have had pork chops tonight. Oh, well, tomorrow is another day. I'm sure gonna send Ulysses Walker for some wine when he gets here. Lend me a half, please."

"Precious Lord, take my hand . . ." Essie began to hum.

"Um-hum!" agreed Laura, "help Sister Essie, Lord, do—so she can help me—because, I swear, for some things I am weak—men, wine, and something fine—just naturally weak."

5

WHEN SAP RISES

"When the sap rises in the trees, it's spring," said Laura. "Babes and boys start holding conferences in which actions speak louder than words. Aw, do it to me, lover!"

"I wish you would not talk that way, Laura, and you supposed to be preparing yourself for the ministry."

"I'm a she-male minister," said Laura, "and there ain't nothing in the Bible says male nor female shall not make love. Fact is, Essie, the very first book is just full of begats, which runs from Genesis through to Tabulations."

"Revelations," said Essie. "I read the Bible when I were a child."

"Which were a long time ago," murmured Laura.

"Just because I'm a few years older than you," said Essie, "you don't need to reflect on it. But if we're gonna start them meetings we been talking about, you ought to start reading up in the Bible."

"Big as that book is, don't nobody know all of what's in it," said Laura. "But I'll take up reading when the time comes. All I need is one text to start me out. And I know one, *Jesus wept*. Also I know another thing He did do. He turned the water into wine—and ever since then somebody's been drunk. Thank God, I seldom go too far."

"Sometimes you guzzle a little too much."

"A little too much is just enough for me—a pint, then I always need just *one* drink more. But what can I do on relief? Not being a street-walker, next best thing to do is be a street-stander—which we gonna be soon as it gets warm enough to stand still long enough in one place to pray."

"Your faith should keep you warm," said Essie.

"My faith and my wine together."

"Laura," cried Essie, "you ain't gonna drink no wine and be standing up preaching God's word beside me, no sir!"

"Are you telling me already what I am and ain't gonna do, Essie, and we ain't even formed our sisterhood yet? You're no relation to me, you know. If we gonna fall out before we start the Lord's work, I'm gonna go right straight and get my two dollars back I put down at Bernstein's on that Bible."

"You done made a payment on the Bible?"

"I did, went right straight and put every penny on it that I won when I caught that first digit the other day—the 4."

"Laura! No you didn't! I don't want to start nothing religious on the wages of sin."

"Wages, hell! I ain't worked a lick since Lincoln's birthday.

That money come from luck. Facts are, it were manna from heaven. I had begun to believe I could not hit a number no more, never in life. Now my faith is restored. Out of gratitude, I paid that two bucks down on a Bible."

"Do, Jesus!" said Essie.

"I could have bought a whole half gallon of wine."

"I know," sighed Essie. Then she went into one of her silent pauses and did not say hardly another word to Laura the rest of the evening. So, when Laura got through looking at Essie's comic books, she went on down the hall to her room and turned the radio on to the all-night record man. Essie just sat and looked at the wall until she got ready to go to bed.

It was warm enough to leave the window open tonight for air. But it was well past the middle of June before the two women thought it warm enough to go seek a corner on which to lift their voices in song and see if anybody stopped to listen. They found at the Good Will Store a tambourine and a folding camp stool, 35¢ for the latter, and a half dollar for the tambourine.

"Including the Bible, we have invested $2.85 in this holy deal," said Laura.

"What we take up tomorrow night, if we does take up anything, goes on the Bible," said Essie.

"Beyond that, we will split it two ways," declared Laura. "A two-dollar payment to Bernstein's ought to leave a little change for the Lord's servants. We have our earthly needs."

"*All* we take up at our first meeting is going on the Bible," said Essie. "Period!"

Never having seen Essie that firm about anything before, Laura opened her mouth to speak, then closed it in surprise, opened it again, and very slowly let it close.

"Tomorrow night at seven at 126th and Lenox," continued Essie. "Leastwise, that's what you said, we raise our hymns. I think I'll wear my coat in case it's chilly."

"Yeah," said Laura, "and we might need that switchblade you keep in your coat pocket to protect our collection on the way back up these dark steps. You never can tell what folks will do when they see we got money."

"Laura, can you play a tambourine?"

"I can play it and *pass it* both," said Laura. "We gonna take up some money."

6

THE CALL

"It were Palm Sunday when I got the call," preached Laura. "I were setting in my room with Sister Essie here, and I heard a voice just as loud saying, 'Take up the Cross and follow Me, go out unto the highways and byways and save souls, go to the curb-stones and gutters and rescue the lost, approach the river of sin and pull out the drowning.' Oh, I were drowning once, friends, but now I'm saved. I were down there in sin's gutter lower than a snake's belly—now look at me! Look at me up here on the curb-stone of life reaching out with my voice to you to come and be saved, too. The Reed Sisters, folks, that's who we are, lifting our voices for God's sake. Our church is this corner, our roof is God's sky, and there's no doors, no place in our church that is not open to you because there is no doors. So come in and be one with us, one with God, and be saved. See how things will change for you—from worst to bad to better to best. Babes and boys, come in! Draw nigh! Men and women, come in! Approach! Children, stand near! Young and old, everybody, drop a nickel, dime, quarter in this tambourine as we sing:

> *"What He's done for me!*
> *What He's done for me!*
> *I never shall forget*
> *What He's done for me!*

"Sing it, Sister Essie, while I shake and pass this tambourine."

Essie's voice rose in happy song while Laura's tambourine trembled and shook in rhythm, and the words and the music spread to the crowd. The fifteen or twenty persons on the corner sang, too. Their singing made others stop to look, stop to sing, and as they sang Laura stopped shaking her music-maker to move among them, the tambourine held like a plate, and the very first nickels, dimes, and quarters bounced into it. Soon the bottom of the instrument was covered, then they didn't bounce any more, they clinked. They clinked into a rising mound which grew heavier and heavier before Laura returned to the camp stool where her tote bag was into which she poured the money.

> *"I never shall forget*
> *What He's done for me!"*

Laura lifted her empty tambourine in an ecstatic shimmer to the power of a song, brought it down trilling and spangling, struck it repeatedly in a drumlike rhythm against her elbow, then shouted "Amen!" Both women led the song to a joyous close, and Laura hissed to Essie, "I think it's time to stop this meeting, girl."

Their first meeting had not begun at seven o'clock as planned. In her room Essie was dressed, ready and waiting, with her old black coat hanging over a chair—but no Laura. Uly *would* come by that afternoon to fool away Laura's time. Laura's room door was locked, and when Essie went down the hall and knocked after the clock hand had passed seven-fifteen, all she got was a "I hear you, Essie! Just wait. I'll be along in due time."

It was after eight when Laura came bouncing up the hall, powdered and grinning, and Essie heard Uly's footsteps going down the stairs. By that time Essie had gone into one of her pauses, just sitting, so was not very communicative as Laura borrowed a slice of cheese from her icebox and chattered as she ate.

"Come on, let's go! Tonight's the night. You have the tambourine and the camp stool? Even if we ain't got a Bible, I got a text, 'Take up your cross and follow Me.' Come on."

"Laura, you're a cross yourself," said Essie.

"Then we'll put up with each other's crosses," laughed Laura. "Get up off your fat bohunkus and let's go see what's cooking with the public. Energize yourself, Essie! You been setting looking at these four walls for the last five or six years. Get up and give out—and see what we get back. Cast your singing bread upon the muddy waters of Harlem this evening, while I pass this tambourine amongst the sinners."

Laura grabbed the secondhand tambourine from the table and started shaking it: *Ching-a-ching! A-ching-ching! Ching-ching-ching!*

"I got that old-time religion!
Got that old-time religion!
That old-time religion—
And it's good enough for me!"

Ching-ching! A-ching-ching! Ching-ching! The way she shook it, it sounded good. The music pulled Essie out of her trance. She picked up the folding stool, threw her coat over her arm, fumbled for her key in her purse, turned out the light, and locked the door. Down the stairs and out into the June night went she and Laura headed for Lenox Avenue and a new life.

Auto horns were honking, taxis flying by, arc lights blinking, people passing up and down the street, restaurants and bars full, wine-o's sitting on a box just around the corner from the grocery store drinking from a common bottle, and nobody stopping for anything when Essie and Laura stopped on the corner they had chosen the day before. There Essie put down her camp stool and laid her coat on it. Laura lifted up her tambourine and shook it. Just the shaking of her tambourine was enough to make a teen-age boy stop, also a middle-aged couple, plus two children who ran past, then ran back and stood watching. Two human pebbles in the Harlem brook had begun to change the course of its water.

For a few seconds Laura shook her tambourine, then she began to sing:

"I got that old-time religion . . ."

As Essie joined in, Laura hit her elbow with the tambourine—one-two! Three-four! in perfect rhythm to the song. Then one of the wine-o's yelled, "Aw, play it, sister!" as he rose unsteadily to participate. And it wasn't a minute before a dozen folks had gathered there on the corner, the two running kids were dancing to Essie and Laura's song, and an elderly woman had three times shouted "Amen!"

"Precious Lord, Take My Hand" followed. Essie prayed. Then Laura announced that it was Palm Sunday when she got the call. And that's the way they started saving souls in Harlem.

7

BIBLE AND BONUS

"This is $11.93 more than we had this afternoon," said Laura when they got home. "Now, I wonder who in hell put them pennies in that tambourine?"

"Blessed is he that giveth, and blessed is he that receiveth," said Essie, "and pennies count, too. Maybe the poor soul did not have any more."

"Yes, but how are we gonna divide up three pennies equal?"

"Divide up?" said Essie. "This is the Lord's money, and we gonna put it all on the Bible—which means we can get the Bible out. We'll only owe five or six more dollars to have it paid for in full."

"I'll be damned," said Laura. "I will put $2 on the Bible—but the rest I need. Here, you take half—six, plus two for the Bible—

which leave me $3.93 for my earthly needs. I'm going downstairs right now with mine before the likker store closes and make an investment—minus what I'm gonna save to play 319 in the morning."

"Laura!"

But Laura had gone on, out the door. Her feet were taking her down the stairs as fast as a child's. Essie sat down on a kitchen chair and went into a pause. In her mind's eye she saw the people stopping on that Lenox Avenue corner to listen to her and Laura sing. Out of their pockets had come this money on the table, and somehow Essie did not think it belonged to her. Essie thought it ought to go in some way to the works of God. So she gathered it up and put it into a spice jar marked CLOVES, on the shelf. The next morning she took it to Bernstein's and turned it in on the Bible, a heavy and beautiful book which she brought home since it was now two-thirds paid for and the store had made its profit. As a bonus, the surprised clerk gave her a little framed motto which said: GOD BLESS THIS HOME. Essie hung it on the wall beside the window.

She sat down and stared at GOD BLESS THIS HOME and whispered, "Send me my daughter home. I know You will. But I got to have a nice place for Marietta to come to first. Lord, I know You will give me that, too." And a still small voice said, "But you've got to get up off this chair and get your feet on the Rock." In her mind's eye the Rock was 126th and Lenox.

And Laura was there, too—Laura, who had managed to pull Essie out of her lifelong trance. Wine-loving, man-loving Laura. "I got to give Laura credit, Lord, for connecting me to You. Not that You wasn't in my mind, Lord, and in my soul—but I hadn't had no direct connections with You since my girlhood. Laura reached out and called Your name, and a prayer come into my mouth then and there. It has stayed murmuring in my heart since Palm Sunday. That Laura lets her prayers float away like soap bubbles and bust. But my prayers stick here, Lord. Here, Lord, here!"

Essie beat a hand against her breast, and thought about Laura right then, no doubt joking with the likker store clerk as she bought a bottle of the cheapest wine—which she would share with whomever she met in the block. Laura would share whatever anybody owned, including herself, Laura, or herself, Essie. Except over men, Laura was not selfish. But a man, if she liked him, she wanted that man for herself alone.

Neighbors for five years. When you're neighbors with people on the same floor in the same kitchenette roominghouse, you learn about them, just being neighbors. Only once in their seven years of friendship had Laura spent the night with Essie. That was the evening when a man who claimed he was real deep in love with Laura and had given her a dress, threatened to whale the living daylights out of her because she did not physically return his love. In fact, right on the public streets the man did bruise her a couple of times by planting his foot twice on the cheeks of Laura's thighs as she switched scornfully away from him in the dress he had bought and paid for. If Laura had not screamed so loudly on the corner, he might have inflicted even more solid punishment on her in places where the bruises would show. At any rate, a passing taxi which drove off with Laura slamming the door saved her before the man could grab the handle. But that night Laura was afraid to go home down the hall to her own room, so she slept with Essie.

For about a year after that a nice young man lived with Laura and was her protector, during which time older Negroes were scarce at Laura's end of the hall. But young men won't do right. They see a young girl and their heads get turned, no matter how nice an older woman is to them. No matter if she does give, rather than take.

When no man was around, Laura seldom liked to cook. Instead, she would put some change in with Essie's change and together they would stew up a pot and both would eat—which was one reason she was in and out of Essie's room so much. That was also why Essie's garbage pail had a wine bottle or two in it almost every day, although Essie herself did not drink. Essie's only bad habit was sitting. Just sitting.

"Girl, a pulpit chair is the very thing for you," said Laura. "You can set whilst I preaches, and you don't even need to get up to sing less'n you want to. When we get our own church, we gonna do just like we want to do."

"Like God wants, you mean," said Essie.

"With His guidance, and *my* mind," said Laura, "and you setting there looking all calm and sweet with not a cloud on your landscape. Essie, you can just set and look more unworried than anybody I ever seen. Me, I need to be doing something—good, bad, or indifferent—but something. No wonder you never has no misfortunes. You just sets."

"I'm setting and thinking on God these days," said Essie. "You better be thinking on Him too, Laura. Take our Bible in your room and read it tonight."

"Can't I read it here?"

"If you want to."

"Where is that part about *begat?*" asked Laura.

8

POINTED QUESTIONS

"Who will come and walk with Him, talk with Him, sing with Him?" Laura cried as old folks, young folks, boys and girls passed up and down the lighted street. But enough paused, lingered, and stood for her and Essie to maintain a crowd. With their backs to the taxis and the passing cars, in the balmy summer air they had conducted a very happy meeting that evening and many voices had joined in their songs—a little unusual for street meetings, where people stopped to *listen* to singing but seldom joined in. Essie and Laura had a way of pulling voices right out of people's throats and getting them to blend with their own in the old songs of the church that everybody knew, or in the more recent gospel songs folks heard on their radios or records. Now, with practice, Laura was beginning to beat a tambourine with rhythms like Cozy Cole's drums.

Playing and singing and talking were the only things about their corner that interested Laura, but these were the least that interested Essie. Sitting on her camp stool while Laura held forth, you'd think Essie had gone into a pause, but this was not true. Her eyes, that seemed to move so slowly, were studying faces, looking into other eyes, wondering what troubled this woman, what worried that man, what had hurt that young boy's soul, or made so bitter that girl's face. Essie, when the meetings were over, would linger and talk to folks until Laura would almost have to drag her away.

"Girl, you don't have to stand on the curb talking to these people all night. Collection is took. Come on! I'm thirsty myself." Laura would start off down the street, walking fast.

Behind her, Essie explaining, "Laura, seems like them folks think I can help them."

"You've done helped yourself. You might *can* help them," says Laura, "but why bother?"

Curving the corner of 125th and Lenox, Essie replies, "Because I think maybe that is the way to help ourselves—by helping others."

"You better help *yourself* first," passing the Lido Bar where the music's coming out. Says Laura, "Smell that fried chicken in there? If this bar wasn't so near our meeting corner, I'd stop and have me a wing and a Bud. That would help me."

"There's nothing wrong with helping somebody else besides ourselves, is there?" persists Essie. "You helped me to pull out. Now look at us, we ain't hardly started in His work, yet already we're prospering in the Lord. This month we don't have to worry."

"Then why worry?" asks Laura. "Don't worry about them folks on that corner after you get their donations. We're straight tonight. Buy yourself some barbecue to take home. I'm gonna get me a quart of the very best sherry wine and get good and high so I can sleep it off. I'm also gonna buy Uly a red sport shirt in the morning, which kind I heard him say he wanted. I like that big old no-good stud myself, I swear I do. If the Lord just takes care of me, I'll take care of my man. Aw, don't look so shocked, Essie! You're out here hustling just like me—in God's name."

"Laura," Essie asks as they cross Fifth Avenue to reach the liquor store on the other side before midnight, "is we doing right?"

"Soon as we're starting to get so we don't have to worry about being wrong, *you* start worrying about being right. Girl, good night! Go on home. I'm gonna stop by Big John's with my bottle and see is Uly playing cards up there. Are we straight on the dough?"

"I don't know," said Essie. "Keep what's in your bag."

"Then don't blame me if I got a dime more than you. And don't let nobody rob you on the way home."

"I got the same knife I been had for twenty years."

"I know it's sharp, so you're all right."

"But I'm worried about what we're doing, Laura. I'm going home and pray."

Laura stopped in her tracks. "Essie, is your wig gone?"

9

ENTER BIRDIE LEE

"All you loose-limbed sons and daughters of Satan, jumping-jacks of sin, throwing your legs every-which-a-way, dancing, letting your feet lead you every-which-a-where, sinning, playing cards by day and fornicating by night, turn! I say turn! Turn your steps toward God this evening, join up with us, and stand up for Jesus on this corner," Laura commanded. "Talk, speak, shout, declare your determination. Who will stand up and testify for Him? If nobody else will, I will—me, Laura Wright Reed. Yes! Yes! I will! Folks, since God took my hand, I have not wanted for nothing. Rent paid, pots full, clothes on my back. Satisfied, praise God! Ain't that right, Sister Essie?"

Essie from her camp stool affirmed, "True, true! Yes, bless God, true!"

Laura continued, "It's God's doings, so I ask you all to help me stay in His footsteps. Help me to stay on the right road, people. Help me, all you-all, until you find the road yourself. Put a nickel, dime, quarter, dollar in this tambourine. Put it here and help in the Lord's work."

"I has done put a quarter in there once," said a little old lady in the crowd, "now I wants to testify."

"Speak, sister, speak," cried Essie.

She came forward, and the little old lady talked so long and so loud that she held up Laura's collection.

"My name is Birdie Lee," she said. "Once I were a child of God, but I backslid, backslid, backslid. Tonight I'm coming home. This evening I makes my determination to stay on His side from here on in—and I mean *into* the Kingdom. Sister Laura, gimme that tambourine and lemme shake it a mite to his glory." Whereupon that little old lady began a song and shook the tambourine—shook it so well that the whole corner started to rock and sway, feet to patting, hands to clapping, and Essie to shouting. So much rhythm swept up and down the street that some of the passing cars slowed to see what was happening—and it made Laura mad. But she did not show it. She sang and clapped her hands, too. But in her soul of souls Laura did not want any other woman on that corner attracting all that attention.

Who in the hell is this Birdie Lee? thought Laura without opening her mouth.

"I'm a sinner determined to be a saint," said Birdie Lee, as if she read Laura's mind. "I'm gonna join up with this band and sing and shout out here on God's street this whole blessed summer long, and nobody's gonna stop me, because—

"I want to be in that number
When the saints go marching in! . . ."

Sister Birdie Lee shook Laura's tambourine and sang the song until all of Lenox Avenue seemed like a street of gold leading right up to God's throne. When she had finished her song and Laura snatched the tambourine out of her hand and started to take up collection, money showered into the instrument. Birdie Lee went and stood beside Essie on the curb and became a part of their church. Because Birdie Lee seemed like a good investment, commercially speaking, Laura did not object.

10

THE FIX

"Some of you-all are going to throw your money away anyhow, so throw some of it here," was the way Laura opened her collection speech one Friday evening. This brought a laugh and filled the tambourine with bills from the sporting element.

"How you can keep your mind on money so much, and on God at all, is more than I can fathom," said Essie gazing at Laura when they got home that night.

"God helps them that helps themselves," said Laura. "I can't help Him if I don't get mine. Them pimps and gamblers and whores on that corner was all headed for the nearest bar or cabaret, anyhow, like I would be if I was them, so why shouldn't I get mine before it goes to the paddys that owns these Harlem guzzle joints? After all, Lenox Avenue is *my* people. Let 'em drop me a little of that money on the way to the bar, instead of it all going right to the white man. Money is color-blind—but you almost have to reach over the color line to get it. Only with the Lord's help did we get what we got here tonight. And you, Essie Belle Johnson, you ain't made so much money before in one day since you been black. Have you?"

"No."

"And whose hand reached out to get it for you?"

"The Lord's."

"And *mine*," said Laura. "These gospel songs is about the only thing the white folks ain't latched onto yet. But they will, soon as they find out there's some dough in 'em. They'll be up here in Harlem running revival meetings on our corner, I expect, in due time. Billy Graham will have a gospel chorus and Mahalia Jackson a white manager. Just you mark my words."

"Can't nobody manage God," said Essie.

"White folks've got the nerve to try," said Laura. "And I don't see nowhere in the Bible where God tells me not to pass my tambourine."

"He driv the money-changers out of the temple," said Essie.

"Money-*changers*," said Laura. "Us is different. We are money-getters."

"I visions trouble," said Essie, and she went into a pause. Sure enough, in the midst of their singing that night a cop walked up and asked Laura if they had a license to be out there on that corner.

Laura said, "This is my license." She reached down in her tote bag and pulled out a greenback which happened to be a ten, and put it in the cop's hand—and that was that. Essie did not miss a note, nor Birdie Lee a handclap, and Laura's tambourine shook louder than ever as the policeman walked away. The next time, a few nights later, he came back with a pal in an ordinary suit, a plainclothes man of the type anybody can spot. At his appearance all the Negroes in the crowd sang louder than ever. The plainclothes man had the feeling that he might have a singing riot on his hands if he went too far, so he accepted a ten, too. But Laura and her tote bag moved off a half block from the meeting for this negotiation, out of the public eye. Meanwhile, Essie clapped the rhythm of a song while the corner continued to jump. The fix was on. For the rest of the summer whenever the Law came by for its cut, Laura would walk a few paces down the block, hand over a bill, and calmly return to her soul-saving.

By the time the summer hurricanes and the late August rains swept the trash from the gutters and the people from the sidewalks, the weather made it unfeasible to meet outdoors some nights. That did not worry Laura. When they did hold a meeting, they took up enough change to last a while.

Essie said, "Laura, what we gonna do when the cold weather comes?"

Laura said, "We'll just find ourselves an inside meeting place. For a couple of hundred dollars under the table, we'll rent some old apartment, buy some secondhand undertaker chairs, and raise a prayer."

"We need a rostrum to put the Bible on, too," said Essie. "I wonder how much does a rostrum cost. In what kind of store do you buy a rostrum?"

11

ETHIOPIAN EDEN

Shortly after the first nip of frost bit the autumn air, Essie Belle Johnson, Laura Reed, and Miss Birdie Lee descended on an old first-floor apartment between Lenox and Seventh in the West 130's with brooms, mops, and pails and proceeded to create that which is next to godliness, cleanliness, in rooms which badly needed cleaning. Three rooms, a bath, and kitchen. A front parlor and a back parlor, with big sliding double doors between, that nobody had used for parlors for years. An old brownstone converted into apartments, the parlors had become bedrooms, until the landlord put a family from Georgia out in response to Laura's under-the-table payment and three months' rent in advance.

When Essie pushed back the tall double doors and made the two big rooms one, she said, "Praise God, this is our church!" She stood like a large angel with her arms stretched out between the double doors and shouted. Whereupon Birdie Lee got to leaping and jumping and shouting, too. But Laura just stood and looked at them. Finally she said, "Saints, we better get to mopping." The next day Laura commissioned a young artist and gave him her instructions.

"I don't care what scenes from the Bible you paint on these windows," said Laura to the artist with the paint cans, "just so you make them colored. I want every last angel you paint to be brownskin. If you put the Devil in, make him white."

"I thought I would put Christ feeding His sheep on one window," said the young artist, "and the woman at the well on the other."

"God made us in His own image," said Laura, "so God must be black, or at least dark brown. As to the lambs, you know what color my Lenox Avenue lambs are."

"Yes'm," said the young man.

"So I look like a ma'am to you?" said Laura.

"No, ma'am, but—"

"I ain't all that age-able," said Laura, who had eyes for that artist. But the painter did not seem interested in anything but his work, and he made two such pretty pictures on the front windows that Laura said, "I think you had better paint me a Garden of Eden on the wall of that back parlor behind where the rostrum is gonna stand. Make me an Eve about the color of Sarah Vaughan. Put a diamond in that serpent's head, and let that apple be a Baldwin. I want Adam to look just like Joe Louis. Champeen! I love that man!" declared Laura. "And let the grass be green, green, green, all around the floor level."

"Yes, ma'am," said the young artist. "I will paint you the prettiest Garden of Eden you ever saw." Which he did.

He also painted the rostrum gold. And he found two big red chairs at the Good Will Store for the Reed Sisters to sit in. He also suggested adding ribbons to their tambourines.

"I love that artist," Laura confided to Essie. "He's got ideas. That young boy could really be my man."

"That boy ain't nothing but a baby," said Essie.

"A sugar baby to me," said Laura.

"There will be no assignations in this church," said Essie flatly. "That back bedroom behind Eden we are going to use as a powder room for the womens, and also as a place to revive them that passes out from shouting. The kitchen we will use for making coffee, tea, cocoa for our church socials. But there will be no beds nowhere."

"I was thinking of moving one in myself," said Laura, "and saving rent by using that bedroom. There's got to be some kind of caretaker here."

"The Lord is the caretaker of this church," said Essie. "Besides, there's a janitor lives downstairs. No need of you living in here all by yourself."

"Just an idea," said Laura. "But where we living now is not fit for servants of the Lord. We've both got to move. Since we got our church—which you just *had* to have first—to find a nice apartment for ourselves is the next step."

"If we prosper here," said Essie, "which I know we will."

"And I do not want no private house," said Laura. "I want a place with an elevator, janitor service, plenty of light, maybe even a doorman like they have on Riverside, everything for comfort."

"You expects to live high on the hog," said Essie.

"We both have chose the higher things of life now," said Laura, "and it's about time. You ain't no spring chicken, you know."

"Don't but a midget span separate you from me, Laura. You just happen to be well preserved, that's all."

"In wine, too," said Laura. "But you know, Essie, I'm developing a taste for Scotch."

"Wine is a mocker and strong drink is a tempter," said Essie.

"Even hard cider's got a kick to it," declared Laura. "When that serpent handed Eve that apple, he probably knew Eve could make hard cider out of it. Aw, look at that beautiful apple that artist-boy's painted for our altar! Pretty enough to eat!"

"Eve do look a lot like Sarah Vaughan," said Essie.

"Ethiopia's Garden of Eden," said Laura. "Listen, I got an idea. For our Sunday school, we gonna have some pretty brown-skin cards printed too—Adam, Eve, the Lord God Jesus, Mary and Mary Magdalene all colored, black, brown, sepia, and mer-iney—with brownskin cherubs that our children can say, 'That's me!' This is gonna be a race church."

"We're colored ourselves," said Essie.

"When we add a man minister to our staff, he's gonna be the biggest blackest coloredest minister I can find," said Laura. "Black to the glory of God, amen!"

"I do not vision no man minister soon," said Essie.

"Then God will have to lift the veil from your eyes," stated Laura, "because male and female created He them—including ministers. So it would do no harm to have a man around now that we got our church."

"Thank God it ain't no little old store-front church neither," said Essie.

"We're eight steps up from the street," said Laura.

"We's rising," said Essie.

Laura sat down in her big red chair at the right of the rostrum in front of the Garden of Eden. She threw one shapely leg over the chair arm and turned to stare up at the bright new picture of the Garden on the wall behind her.

"Aw, just look at Joe Louis—Adam—naked as a kangaroo behind that bush—and he's peering out at Eve! Look at Joe!"

"Adam: *man*—that's what Adam means," said Essie, *"man."*

"Joe sure God is a man!" said Laura.

12

DYED-IN-THE-WOOL

The first convert in the new church was a man, a *real sinner*, too, not just a backslider returning to the fold. He was an old sinner who had been sinning for a long, long time. His name was Crow-For-Day—Chicken Crow-For-Day. He stood against the Garden of Eden and declared his determination.

It was a warm October evening and the front windows with the dusky lambs painted on them were open, so people in the street could hear him as he cried his new-found strength; and voices even outside the windows said "Amen!"

It was their first Sunday night in the new church. Laura was proud, Essie was happy, and their joy and happiness radiated to all the people. It was the first service they had ever held with a piano, too, and the young man who played had a rhythm and a roll that sent waves of jubilant sound rippling up and down the aisles between the folding chairs and bouncing off the walls and ceiling. Somebody said that Eve in the picture, at a certain point, even started to open her mouth and sing, and the snake gave a couple of wiggles. And at one place in the Sunday services, maybe because she was thinking about her daughter in the South, Essie was moved to stand and sing all alone "Sometimes I Feel Like a Motherless Child" and people started to cry, and Chicken Crow-For-Day jumped up and said, "I'm motherless and fatherless, too, but right now this minute I know I have found Jesus."

He shouted until Essie finished singing, then the old man took the rostrum and began to testify.

"Right now this minute I have come to God!" He was six feet tall, acknowledged sixty years old, thin as a shadow, and he said, "Right now I have found God! After all my years of sin, tonight the light!"

So many people in the church shouted simultaneously that you could hardly hear Crow-For-Day. But he went on, "Dyed-in-the-wool, dyed-in-the-wool, a dyed-in-the-wool sinner, dyed-in-the-wool with a dye so deep and a stain so dark that only the lamb of God could wash me clean. I seen these lambs in these windows and I said I'm going in. And I come—and look at me now, white, whiter than snow, washed white!" And nobody laughed that he was not white at all, because everybody was listening beyond his words and looking through him to the hope that they, too, might find some sort of joy akin to his, some kind of sin cleanser, though it be but for a moment, like this ancient reprobate had found—for you could look into his face and tell he had been until this moment a hound.

"Sniffing after women, tailing after sin, gambling on green tables, Saratoga, Trenton, High Point, North Carolina, let 'em roll! Santa Anita, Hialeah, Belmont, Miami, never read nothing but the racing forms. Harlem, nothing but the numbers columns in the *Daily News*. And for relaxations, crime in the comic books. Oh, but tonight Sister Essie has done snatched me off the ship of iniquity on which I rid down the river of sin through the most awfullest of storms, through gales of evil and hurricanes of passions, purple as devil's ink, green as gall. Yes, I tell you I shot dices. Now I've stopped. I lived off of women. Uh-uh! No more! I'll make my own living now. I carried a pistol, called it Dog—because when it shot, it barked just like a dog. I won't carry no pistol no more. Looky here! Everybody, looky here!"

Four women fainted and twenty screamed as Crow-For-Day pulled a pistol from his pocket, walked down the aisle with it above his head, and threw it out the open window into the street. Pistol out the window, gone.

"I carried a knife. Knives got me in trouble. Here goes old knife, too." And out the window went the knife, gone. As heavy as Essie was, she leaped into the air three times on the rostrum and said, "Thank God!"

"I hope, Essie, you'll throw your old switchblade away, too," said Laura on the platform but Essie did not hear her at all, or if she heard, she did not reply.

By then Crow-For-Day had come back up the aisle to the front of the church and turned to reveal still more of his sinful past to the congregation. "I drank likker," he shouted.

"Me, too," said Sister Birdie Lee.

"It made me fool-headed," cried Crow-For-Day. "Thank God I stopped last year so I don't have to stop drinking now."

"We stopped, stopped, stopped," said Birdie Lee.

"Let the man talk, Birdie," said Laura. "Let the new soul talk."

"I witnessed the chain gang," cried Chicken, "the jail, the bread line, the charity house—but look at me tonight. Look at me now!"

"Look, look, look," cried Birdie Lee.

"Bless God, I've lived to see the rooster crow for day, the sun of grace to rise, the rivers of life to flow—and I have found my determination. Help me! Help me! Brothers and sisters, help me."

Whereupon, Laura came forward with a singing cry, took the convert's hand, and appealed to the congregation on Crow-For-Day's behalf:

> *"When you see some sinner*
> *Leave iniquity's dark den*
> *And turn his feet toward Canaan,*
> *Friends, help him to begin.*
> *Christians, take his hand,*
> *Show him God's his friend,*
> *Just lead him on*
> *And say Amen!"*

The building began to rock to the song. Shaking hands and dancing feet laced the rhythm into a net of ecstasy while the piano bassed its chords of confirmation.

> *"Let the church say Amen!*
> *Let the church say Amen!*
> *When a sinner comes to Jesus*
> *Let the church say Amen!"*

13

LIKKER AND LOOT

"I got two thousand dollars in that spice jar in the cupboard," said Essie, "so I think we better take it to the bank."

"I think so, too," said Laura, "to the colored bank."

"To the Carver," said Essie.

"Yes, because that's too much loot to keep in the house any more. Who'd've ever thought this time last year, you and me would be banking money?"

"You have shook your tambourine to blessings," said Essie.

"I'm gonna shake it to a mink coat by Christmas," declared Laura, inspecting an unopened bottle of Scotch.

"I'm gonna shake mine to glory," said Essie.

"You are doing right well shaking since you bought your own

self a tambourine, too. But I'm still the champion shaker—and collection taker."

"You do all right, Laura, and you deserves to buy a nice Christmas present for yourself. I wonder will I have my daughter with me by then?"

"You said you wanted to wait till we got an apartment, didn't you? A nice place to bring her to, not this old run-down joint. Essie, suppose we take this two thousand dollars and move, instead of putting it in the bank?"

"No, Laura. The church needs a nest egg. This is it. We put this away. Then maybe we start doing a little something for ourselves."

"O. K., as you say. I'm happy—I got my man to keep me warm."

"Looks like you could choose a new man out of the church."

"This one is just temporary, honey."

"Must be, 'cause I ain't even met him."

"He comes in early and goes out late," said Laura. "Lemme get on down the hall and see is he there yet."

"You gave him a key?"

"Sure—which is why I told you to keep our money in *your* room. You know I'm generous with my keys. Why, that key-man around the corner has made me so many keys to my door he must know its shape by heart."

"Ain't you scared someone of them mens will open your door some night and catch you with somebody else?"

"Don't worry, Essie, I got a night latch inside, also a bolt. Besides, when I put a man down, they usually don't fool around no more, key or no key, especially now—since they think I can put the curse of God on their sinful souls, me being a lady minister. Negroes don't play around with the church much. They take it serious."

"I wish you'd take it serious yourself," said Essie.

"As if I don't," exclaimed Laura. "But you won't catch me lending no money to nobody in the church, like you did Sister Birdie Lee last week. Facts is, I don't think you ought to start it."

"Birdie Lee paid me back."

"You're lucky. I expect she borrowed it to buy herself a tambourine."

"No, she didn't. She borrowed it to get a tooth pulled."

"Birdie's trying to tambourine herself up on the rostrum with us," said Laura, "setting in the front row playing like mad."

"She sure can shake it," confirmed Essie. "She tells me she can play drums, too. When we get our orchestra we planning, let's give her a chance."

"Essie, do you want to help every stray we pick up—and put them in the forefront, too? Let Birdie Lee set down there in the congregation where she belongs. Dried up and ugly as Birdie is, nobody wants to look at her."

"No, but her music's a different thing. Nobody wants to look at me neither, much, fat as I am, but they like to hear me sing. You are the rose of this church."

"Thank God for making me a high-breasted woman," said Laura. "But what you're probably thinking, though, is—I can tell by looking at you—that *you* are the saint and I am the devil. Well, fool, go ahead on and work and pray and worry yourself down with their problems if you want to. Lend out your money. Kill yourself over that church. Not me."

"Laura, the needs is so big up here in Harlem, and the ways of helping so little, I figure we have to work hard," said Essie.

"How come, after all these years I've knowed you, just *this* year you find so much energy all of a sudden?"

"From God," said Essie.

"With *me* propelling," said Laura.

"You God's handmaiden—even if you do not always act like a holy maiden do."

"How does a holy maiden act?" asked Laura.

"They be's not bold with their sinning," said Essie.

"It's easier for me to be a saint than to be a hypocrite. And neither my light nor my headlights will I hide under a bushel. The Lord gimme these breasts and if they look like headlights on a Packard car, it is not my fault. 'Let your light so shine,' is my belief."

"You would have led that little young artist-boy what painted our church windows to sin if you could."

"I don't believe that boy was leadable, Essie. He were of the type you call 'refined.' But he sure painted a *de*-lightful Garden of Eden. Even that serpent looks like he can be persuaded! Oh, well, lemme see if this English White Horse tastes as good as that Johnny Walker I had last night. I'm trying all the different brands of Scotch to see which one I'm gonna settle on for life. I can see my picture in a magazine now—when I get to be as famous at soul-saving as was Aimee Semple McPherson—*Sister Laura Reed endorses Vat 69 as ideal for colds and fevers, nothing else.* I will get five thousand dollars for that endorsement."

"Your mind sure runs to likker and to loot," said Essie. "But one of these days the Spirit is going to strike you dry, strike greed from your heart, lust from your body, and—"

"Make me as stupid as you are," Laura cut her off, "without a idea in your head until I put this one there—that's brought us a good living. Now you want to cramp my style."

Essie could tell Laura was angry. Suddenly the tone of voice hurt, her eyes cut, and Essie suffered. She sat down in her chair and said no more. When Laura left with her Scotch, Essie went into a pause.

14

ENTER BUDDY

He just walked down the aisle out of nowhere, confronted Laura, and spoke. "I saw you on the curb before you moved off the street into this church, and you certainly looked good to me."

"I did not observe you in the services tonight, did I?" asked Laura. She went toward the switch to turn out the altar lights.

"No, I just wandered in after things was over. I saw the people going out. I wondered where you had disappeared to off of Lenox Avenue. Cold weather, naturally you had to go somewhere. I traced you here."

"The Reed Sisters is flattered."

"No *sisters* to it. It's you I'm talking to. Maybe I could ride you somewhere, now that your night's work is done."

"You got a car?"

"I can call a taxi."

"I usually go for a little drink after services," smiled Laura.

"You're a woman after my own heart," grinned the young man. "I'm Buddy—Big-Eyed Buddy."

"And I'm Miss Laura Reed."

"I know. How about your partner who's shaking hands at the door? Does she drink?"

"No, she goes home like she ought to. Essie's the serious type."

"Essie looks it," said Buddy.

Valance lights out over Eden, cluster lights out on the walls, all lights out except at the door.

"Essie, you take the bag. I'm going riding with this young man for an hour. Mrs. Johnson, meet Mr. Buddy—"

"Lomax," said Buddy taking Essie's hand which had—for him—no grip.

"Hey! Taxi!"

The cab stopped and they rode down to the Roma Gardens. Buddy went to the Men's Room and when he came back, seated in her tiny booth Laura looked up, and there at the edge of the table stood a six-foot, a tower-tall, a brownskin, a large-featured, a big-handed, handsome lighthouse-grinning chocolate boy of a man.

"How old are you?" zoomed around the table. However, neither asked the question. But that is what Laura was asking in her mind of him, Buddy in his mind of her. In her mind Laura lied, "Thirty-two." Of him in her mind Laura guessed, "Twenty-four."

In his mind Buddy thought, "Forty—but *forty*," which, accented, meant O. K.

"You're forty with me," he said aloud.

"Forty with me, too, baby," said Laura. "Set down."

Nice lights in the Roma Gardens. Cozy in the Roma Gardens. Out of the way, the Roma Gardens. Whee-ooo-oo-o! How many times in the Roma Gardens! Just as if it never happened to her anywhere before the Roma Gardens. Just as it had happened from there to the Shalimar to Eddie's to the Champagne Bar on the Hill for Buddy.

"I got news for you, I'm married," lied Buddy.

"Which makes me no difference," said Laura.

But Buddy knew it did—older women liked younger men better if they were married—spice to make the pot more tasty, age to make cheese more binding, phosphorus the light more blinding—mellow.

No, not that rat trap where I live, thought Laura. It's got to be some place fine, like the Theresa. Besides, Uly might be—

"What you drinking?"

"White Horse 69," said Laura.

"You kinder mixed up there, aren't you, kid?" Buddy grinned.

"Any kind of good Scotch," Laura laughed.

"House of Lords," the waiter smiled. "Chasers?"

"Ginger ale," Laura said.

"Give her water," Buddy laughed. "She don't know."

Laura didn't laugh. She wanted to know. "Just straight might be safer," she sighed.

"I always play it straight," vowed Buddy.

Juke box not too loud. Bar not too full, no crowd, just right to be not lonesome-looking. Knees not too close, just possible to touch. Table not too wide for a whisper to drift across. If a woman were to whisper, it could drift across. Lights not too bright, yet not too dim to see her eyes, his eyes. And table not too wide for what *what* to drift across?

The *what* that sparks the diamond in the serpent's head?

That painter-boy, remembered Laura. Thank God, Buddy is not *refined!*

Bang-bang-bang across the table the *what* that lights the diamond in the serpent's head.

15

ENTER MARTY

"**Y**ou could sell Holy Water from the Jordan on Sundays and get a Cadillac," said Buddy. "Let's phone down for breakfast."

Below on Seventh Avenue the uptown traffic hummed through the morning sunlight.

"Bishop Lawson's sure got a great big church," said Laura looking out the double windows before coming back to bed. "How much does Holy Water cost?"

"Just turn the tap," said Buddy, "that's all. And I can get you a hundred gross of empty bottles for a little or nothing, with labels: HOLY WATER—a green river and some palms, you know—about the size of dime store Listerines."

"But you mean the water ain't really holy?"

"It's holy if you bless it," said Buddy. "You can rename the Hudson yourself."

"Essie would have a conniption fit," cried Laura. "Hey, chocolate boy with the coconut eyes, what do you want for breakfast?"

"A little Scotch, a stack of wheats, and a little more loving from you," purred Buddy.

Elevators going up and down. Voices in the hall.

"They got a radio station in this hotel," said Laura.

"WLIB," said Buddy. "Ever been interviewed on it?"

"Never."

"Want to be?"

"What should I say?"

"Pray one of your pretty prayers," said Buddy, "like you used to do on the corner. Sing one of your pretty songs. You might get a week at the Apollo on the Gospel Caravan."

"Essie would drop dead," said Laura.

"Rape Essie!" said Buddy.

Grinding of brakes in the street below as a too-fast car comes to a sudden stop.

"How much should we sell it for?" asked Laura.

"What?" said Buddy.

"The Holy Water," Laura pursued.

"A dollar a bottle." Thus the price was set. "A bottle and a label will cost you about two cents. See the profit? See the Caddy by Christmas? Hum-mm-m! Baby, you're built—no false brassieres!"

"Naturally not. Ouch! Buddy, what I want is an apartment."

"I'll call up Marty."

"Who's Marty?"

"The fixer, the man behind the men *behind* the men. Get you anything."

"Colored?"

"You know he *can't* be colored," said Buddy.

"I hear there're six hundred applications for those twenty apartments in that new building on the Hill."

"Marty'll get your application on the very top."

"I never did put in no application."

"Then he'll just get you the apartment," said Buddy.

"Money under the table?"

"Marty don't need money." White sheet, raw chocolate-brown, that Buddy without pajamas.

I got to get me some nice silk nightgowns, thought Laura, at least to put on to take off.

"Marty knows about your church," said Buddy. "You might never see Marty, but he knows about you."

"Just *who* is Marty?"

"The man."

"What man?"

"Behind the throne of Harlem," said Buddy. "And sitting in your bathroom, too."

"What?"

"All over your bathroom," said Buddy.

16

THE DEVIL'S HAM

The winter prospered them. Their two-parlor church grew until so many people wanted to attend that it could no longer hold them all and when the new young leaves were coming out in the spring, Essie found herself standing at a window high up on the ninth floor of a brand-new apartment house looking out over the prettiest edge of Harlem.

"The park! And the river down there!" said Essie. "Laura, how in God's name did you ever get this apartment for us?"

"Buddy—through Marty," said Laura. "Don't frown up—because otherwise we never would have had it. Now you can send for your daughter."

"Thank God for this ham, even if the Devil did bring it!" Essie joked—an old slavery-time joke, it was about a black mother who taught her son that it was a sin to steal; if you did steal the Devil was in you. But they were both hungry and the master's smokehouse was full of hams. So one night the son took a ham from the white man's smokehouse, ran back past their cabin, and threw the ham in the window. The black mother cried, "Thank God for this ham—even if the Devil brung it!" And they ate the ham.

Essie loved the apartment. All she moved out of her old place was her motto: GOD BLESS THIS HOME. It didn't go very well with the modernistic couches and things Laura put in the parlor, but Essie hung it firmly on the wall, nevertheless, and there it stayed.

It was a big apartment. Essie had a bedroom and Laura had a bedroom. There was a dining room, an alcove room, a pantry, and a kitchen. The alcove could be a bedroom, too. They paid cash for the furniture, all the fine new furniture, and it only took two weeks' collections at church. They had six girls now passing tambourines, besides the marching-up collection at the end.

"The Lord has blessed us indeed," said Essie. But the holy services were not unalloyed. For some reason, Birdie Lee was a nightly thorn in Laura's side—and Buddy was a thorn in Essie's. Birdie Lee could sing too loud to be a little woman, and the way she played the drums—they had a small combo in the church now—excited the worshipers to a frenzy and took the spotlight—had there been a spotlight—off of Laura. Without a personal spotlight, Laura was lost, whereas Essie's sweet placidity continued to glow, even as attention shifted. She just sat like a rock to which the bird of public affection continually returned. That downtown columnist who had come to Harlem to hear their singing had mentioned Essie and Birdie Lee in the paper, and wrote not a word about Laura. Marty had sent the man up there to do a funny piece about the Holy Water from Manhattan's Jordan.

That was the rub with Essie—Buddy's ideas came from the Devil. And Buddy was the Devil's shadow—Marty's Harlem handyman. Marty nobody had ever seen. That Holy Water had caused Essie to go into a series of pauses that lasted for days. It had happened long before they moved to the new apartment. When Buddy brought a dozen cases of empty little bottles with colorful stickers on them to their third-floor tenement, for some reason, maybe because Essie's room was nearest the steps, Laura wanted to pile the cases in her room and fill the bottles from *her* sink. But, in Laura's own words, "Essie pitched a bitch."

"After you left, Buddy," Laura related, "she pitched a bitch. 'Take them lying vessels out of here,' she hollered. And Essie would not let me run a drop of water from her sink. Essie said she wouldn't have no parts of this Holy Water jive—when she knew it didn't come from the Jordan, but right out of a New York tap. As for blessing it, Essie said she hoped the Lord would strike me dead if I blessed such low deceit. Oh, well, Essie's getting old. So I got all them bottles corked up in my room, ready for you to take over to the church, case by case, as we need them. Essie says she won't even set on the rostrum while I sell them, so I told her to go mediate in the backroom then while the selling ceremony is going on—it being *my* rostrum as well as hers. She allows as how she will not only mediate, but pray for my soul."

"That Essie's too holy for her own good," said Buddy.

But that is exactly what happened—on the nights when Laura sold Holy Water for a dollar a bottle, Essie withdrew to the bedroom behind the Garden of Eden and got down on her knees and prayed for the serpent to drop its apple of greed. In her mind Buddy was the serpent.

"How simple can people get," scorned Buddy, "buying Holy Water from the Jordan at a buck a bottle! Ha-ha! Always looking for some kind of lucky stuff here in Harlem. I depend on *myself,* myself."

"Me, too," said Laura. "But Essie depends on God—and *me.* Without me and my ideas where would she have been? Still on relief!"

Yet Essie would touch none of the money from the sale of Holy Water. So Laura told her, "All right, then, I'll put it on a Cadillac car." And she did. She bought a car.

LIGHTS OUT

Smoldering coals plus quick young sparks produce murky fires beneath the grills of love. Laura had purchased her new nightgowns. But even in her cold old room before they moved, Buddy did not wear pajamas, never. "I sleep too restless," he said. Meanwhile Laura had changed the lock on her kitchenette door before she moved, and she had stopped giving out keys. Only one to Buddy, and a key to the Cadillac for him when the car was delivered. After all, Buddy had gotten her—and Essie— the apartment to move into as soon as the building would be completed. Oh, happy moving day!

"I'm your stick man," said Buddy, brown head on white pillow with a white cigarette between his chocolate lips. "I've got your extra dice up my sleeve. The Reed Sisters, ha! Some nerve! The greatest gospel team in the business. Got to give it to you-all! And you're the slick one—I admire you, kid. But any angles you women don't know, or can't work, Laura, leave to Papa Buddy."

"Chocolate boy with the coconut eyes," cooed Laura, "kiss me."

"I just got through kissing you," said Buddy. "Listen, Marty give me a new idea for you-all the other day."

"You told me about us maybe doing TV programs with the chorus, and getting our gospel quartet on the air, building them up for a night club act after we get our bigger church."

"Naw, not that," said Buddy, offering Laura a puff from his Camel. "Something easier."

"What?"

"Numbers."

"What do you mean, numbers?" cried Laura. "We can't write no numbers in the church."

"Not write 'em, baby, just pronounce 'em," drawled Buddy.

"Pronounce them?"

"Give numbers out in services. You know, you-all got a mighty big following here in Harlem, and when you move to that old theatre you'll have a bigger—"

"Do you think we're really gonna get that empty old theatre? I hear it's condemned."

"Leave it to Marty. With a white man to front for you, baby, you can get anything. Leave it to me and Marty. Marty can get your records played on the air. Marty can get you a lot of recording dates, and he knows a juke box combine. You'll be interviewed on Doc Wheeler's Gospel Show, aw, baby you'll go places. Now, if you'd just eliminate Essie."

"Buddy, we—"

"O. K., skip it. But I'm going to start working on this record deal soon. The Ward Sisters have sold a million copies of their records. So did Mahalia. With a thousand-seat theatre to fill—"

"Church," corrected Laura.

"Church to fill—you gonna need a bigger draw than just singing and praying. Let the word get around that you give out lucky digits every Sunday—and it will be full."

"Buddy, Essie wouldn't even let me mention numbers in our pulpit."

"You won't need to mention numbers. But, anyhow, we gonna have to get rid of Essie—in due time. She's too straight. In fact, she's so straight, she's square. But right now, that's neither here nor there. You won't have to mention numbers, not in the gambling sense. You just give out some holy hymns from the pulpit, or Bible texts with three numbers, that's all, and let the folks write the numbers down. What happens after that is not your business, nor Essie's. If they play 'em, then they play 'em. See, I'll get the bartenders and the poolhall boys to spread the word around that one of your figures hit for big money the very next week, whether it did or not. From then on, your church will be packed, believe me, baby."

"Big-Eyed Buddy, boy, you got an idea," said Laura kissing him square on the lips as his cigarette in his enormous hand hung over the side of the bed.

"Marty's idea," said Buddy. "Him and his syndicate back the biggest numbers bank in Manhattan. But lately business has been slow, particularly in Harlem. High prices and everything, folks are not playing as much as they used to. It needs a shot in the arm—like Marty's uncle says that minister back in the twenties, who used to give out lucky numbers in his pulpit, gave the whole setup. Hundreds of Harlem saints took down the numbers of his hymns—Lucky Hymns—every Sunday and played them all week long. Get the point?"

"Um-hum," hummed Laura. "If that minister had lucky hymns, I could have texts—Lucky Texts."

"Laura Reed's Lucky Texts," mused Buddy. "And each time you give out a text, pass the tambourine for a quarter, else the players won't be lucky the next day."

"And I wouldn't get mine either," said Laura, "without the tambourines."

"Baby, that'll add a few more hundreds regular to the bank account every week—and the government can't tax no church income."

"Amen!" said Laura.

"Amen's right, baby," purred Buddy, putting an electric arm around her neck and drawing her close. "I want you to get me a red Caddy, sports model, convertible."

"Ain't one Cadillac in the family enough, sugar?"

"I never did like dark-colored cars like yours," he murmured, rolling over. "How about it, baby? You know damn well I got a birthday next month."

"Well, maybe . . ."

Without moving his lips from hers, Buddy reached up to turn out the light at the head of the bed, so Laura did not finish her sentence.

18

STRAY CATS, STRAY DOGS

"Into my church, yes. Into my home, maybe. But into my bed, no!" said Essie squatting on a kitchen chair in their new apartment. "I takes no stray cats."

"If you're gonna throw a hint, throw it clean," said Laura. "I know you're talking about Buddy."

"He's too good-looking to be any good, anyhow," said Essie. "That boy was cut out for a pimp."

"He's got higher ideas," said Laura. "In fact, he's got more than ideas. He's got get-up-and-go, do something about things—which is more than some people I know ever had. Besides, Buddy's no stray cat. He's young, he's healthy, he's smart, he's clean."

"But he ain't no saint. If he's so interested in our church, why don't he get religion?"

"Converted? Buddy?" Laura started to laugh. Then she said, thoughtfully, "He would if I told him to."

"You're not the one to do the telling," said Essie. "That's the spark that comes from God."

"Through me and you in our temple," said Laura, "I believe I'll spark up a few sparks and see what I can do with Buddy."

"You know," mused Essie, "I took in a stray dog once, so frisky and friendly in the street, and clean-looking. After I had him two or three days around home—this were down in Richmond—I found out that that dog had everything a hound could have. He was so frisky and leaped and jumped so much because he had worms. He scooted and slid across the floor so funny because he had the itching piles. He sneezed so cute because he had distemper. Also he had fleas. Besides, when I took that dog to the vet's and paid out my good ten dollars, the man said he had a patch of ringworm behind his ear, which is catching to children and humans. I had to get rid of that dog I had taken into my home. Another time I took a kitten borned of an alley cat, but cute. That kitten grew up to claw one of my neighbor's children in the face, bit me, and had a temper like a tiger. Stray cats, stray dogs, stray people, you can never tell about 'em," said Essie. "You can never tell."

"We got a church full of 'em," said Laura, "and ain't but one turned out bad—that boy that used to come damn near every night to sing and pray, then would go off down the street and light a fire in somebody's house and try to burn them up. Thank God, he never lit no fire in our church before they caught him. I would hate to see my Garden of Eden burnt up."

"When peoples is under the spell of Christ, they most in generally behaves themselves," stated Essie. "But even religion do not touch every heart in time to save it from a life of hellishness and hell. Look how long it took Crow-For-Day to get converted and do right—in his sixty-fifth year before he found salvation—because he told me himself he lied when he said he was only sixty on the night of his conversion."

"Crow's a right good old deacon, even if he did start out his first testimony with a lie. But what's a year more or less? If I told my right age, some folks would be startled."

"Big-Eyed Buddy, for instance," said Essie.

"Lay off my king-size Hershey bar," said Laura. "Buddy's gonna be my business manager."

"You can have him," said Essie.

"My idea man! That boy's got ways of making loot I ain't never knew existed—also of making love. And if I have my way I'm gonna wrap him up in money like a Hershey bar is wrapped in tin foil."

"Loot, loot, and likker, his speed!"

"Unholy trinity," said Laura. "I think I ought to bring that man to the fold. Imagine what a shouting there would be if Buddy got converted some Sunday!"

"What about Monday?"

"Meaning by that?"

"You should be as good on Monday as you are on Sunday."

"Buddy *is* sort of untamable like, ain't he?"

"Stray cats, stray dogs, stray people!" said Essie.

"But are you forgetting what we said in the beginning, Sister Saintly—that our aim was to save them *lower* down than us?" asked Laura. "You done got on a mighty high horse of late, Miss Essie. I hope you don't be riding for a fall."

Having the last word and already at the door, Laura withdrew, breasts higher than ever, head higher still.

19

GOD'S MARQUEE

"Not quite a year," said Laura, dusting off the Bible preparatory to evening services, "and already we got a little church and a big apartment. Soon we gonna have a big church. Essie, I signed the lease on that old showhouse today."

"It look mighty rundown to me."

"They gonna paint it up, turn the stage into a rostrum, and put our names in big lights outside where it used to say JOAN CRAWFORD IN THE LOVES OF PASSION, or some such jive. We're gonna fix up that big room down under the stage for the robing room. And you and me'll have dressing rooms down there, too, when they get 'em built. But I guess I can robe with the choir at first—except we ain't gonna call it a choir no more after we move. We gonna call it the Tambourine Chorus, and our church the Tambourine Temple."

"Which was whose idea?" asked Essie.

"Buddy's," said Laura. "He's an idea man! We're gonna get two pianos, one on either side of the stage—rostrum—and everybody in the chorus will have a tambourine."

"I bet Birdie'll buy herself a new set of drums."

"She'll pay for 'em herself, too," said Laura, "much as she has to run to the toilet during services. That woman must have had a busted bladder once."

"Birdie Lee had a hard life before she come back to Jesus," said Essie.

"She's one of your stray cats for true," said Laura.

" 'Our church has no doors,' you stated yourself out there on that corner, Laura."

"There comes that little old varmint of a Birdie Lee now," said Laura. "Look, she's heading straight up the side aisle, I'll bet toward the bathroom."

"Birdie's always ahead of time for services. Good evening, Sister Lee."

"Good evening, all. I'll see you in a minute. When you got to go, you got to go!" Birdie disappeared behind the Garden of Eden and down the back hall.

"Birdie's being cute," said Laura. "And she never did buy one of my bottles of Holy Water yet."

"Birdie ain't so simple," said Essie. "She knows the score."

"Look, people coming already. Why don't you raise a hymn, Essie, while I go back and make myself a pot of coffee. I neglected to eat my supper tonight."

"Out riding?"

"Yes, out riding—in my Cadillac."

Laura disappeared as Sister Essie went down on the floor level to shake hands with the folks who were coming in. "Sister Jenkins, howdy! . . . Mrs. Longshaw, how you been? . . . Brother Bullworth, good evening to you! . . . Deacon Crow-For-Day, come in! . . . God bless you, Sister Jones."

"Blessed assurance, Jesus is mine!
Oh, what a fortress of glory divine! . . ."

On the day when they moved their church into the renovated theatre, as soon as their numerous members got off from work almost everybody turned out to help, and Deacon Crow-For-Day carried the Bible. Laura carred the rostrum in her big new Cadillac with Buddy driving. Essie took the bus up to the old reconverted theatre which, sure enough, had their names up in great big lights: THE REED SISTER'S TAMBOURINE TEMPLE with the possessive in the wrong place. Nobody noticed that. Besides it was day-dusk so the lights were not yet on.

"God's marquee," said Buddy, "with your name on it—Reed. You're a businesswoman, kid, runner-up to Rose Meta—without having to bother with heads."

"I once thought of going into the beauty business," said Laura. "Never could get the capital. I'm glad I didn't now."

"You'd of been a beauty," complimented Buddy.

"Sweet daddy, I'd kiss you if we wasn't in front of the church."

One thousand seats, and each seat bottom folded back. A balcony that used to be for smoking, but no more. "I wonder if we'll fill the upstairs?" asked Laura.

"Try them Lucky Texts," Buddy advised.

"I'll have to spring that deal on Essie by surprise," said Laura. "I better not do it the first Sunday night. I want a little peace for the dedication."

"You got enough on your program for the opener. Save the Bible luckies for next week," Bud counseled. "Start your shot in the arm on another go-round. Get up there on the rostrum now and lemme see how you look."

Laura mounted the stage. They had rented an enormous golden curtain as a background for the chorus.

"I'm gonna get me a red robe to wear up here," said Laura, "and a purple one to change off. Essie's so big, let her wear black for sin, or white for goodness."

"Baby, you would look gorgeous with nothing on," cried Buddy from the back of the auditorium. "And when that spot-light strikes you . . ."

Essie came panting in and looked around the vast playhouse. "They did clean it up right nice for us, didn't they? And the rostrum looks wonderful with that gold velvet drape. But I miss our Garden of Eden."

"Adam's here," said Buddy, pointing a thumb at himself, "and yonder's Eve."

Laura laughed, but Essie wilted silently into a folding seat at the back and went into a pause, a heaviness in her heart. The other saints were bustling around inspecting the place, and Deacon Crow-For-Day proudly placed the Bible on the rostrum which Buddy eventually brought down to the stage. Birdie Lee emerged from the bathroom and set up her drums, took out her sticks, and rolled a jolly gospel roll. Whereupon, in the darkened auditorium, Essie came to life and cried, "Amen!"

20

STRONG BRANCH

Now in their new apartment, they each had big, beautiful bedrooms. Essie slept alone. Laura—well, there were men's coats hanging in Laura's closet, and male pajamas in her laundry—not for sleeping—pajamas with a red B embroidered in silk on the jacket pocket. Naturally they belonged to that big *black* Negro (which is what Laura called him when she got mad— otherwise he was *dark brownskin*) by name of Buddy. Buddy said he liked the shower with the glass doors in the bathroom, which is why he often slept at their place, just so he could get up in the morning and take a shower.

Essie said "Huh!" at that one.

Water! Wonderful water, cleanliness next to godliness! Buddy was clean, teeth shining, nails polished, Sugar Ray's Barber Shop giving his hair a gleam. Sharp-moving like a boxer, like a beast. Tiger of a boy! Coconut eyes, hair which crackled sometimes when Laura ran a comb through it. For Laura, who had never touched the Holy Grail, Buddy was the nearest thing to such a vessel.

"I thrills when I touches the Bible," said Essie.

"I thrill when I touch that man," grinned Laura.

But it was in their new apartment in the late watch of evening that an unsmiling Laura often poured too many drinks. And it was in the late watch of evening that she occasionally talked too much—or rather too freely, for she always talked. But especially on nights when Buddy was not there, she would go to the case in the pantry and pull out another bottle if the built-in cabinet in the living room was dry. In the day, before services, Laura seldom, if ever, drank. But nighttime, with Buddy off somewhere, the hours were so long!

Essie, being a sleepyhead, seldom kept her company. Essie's new Beautyrest mattress in the big cool bedroom in the new apartment was too comfortable! Besides, she had her books to read, slowly going through the whole Bible, plus Howard Thurman with his rolling sentences concerning Jehovah God, and Norman Vincent Peale telling people how to behave themselves easily. But sometimes Laura would start one of her glass-in-hand talking jags early, before Essie turned in, and it was hard for Essie to be so impolite as to go to bed in the middle of an exposition. When Laura was even just a little drunk, her conversations had a way of weaving continuous links that had no end—for in truth, the end was not yet. Tonight Laura was talking about her mother. It had begun with the lighted cross in the living-room panel which Laura said the writer from *Ebony* that afternoon had called a *symbol*. "And I thought a *cymbal* was something on a drum," said Laura.

"Crosses and nothing else holy don't mean a thing if you don't live right," said Essie, "whatever you may call 'em. And you, Laura, singing and preaching and praying in church half the night and drinking at home the rest, you are burning your candle at both ends."

"My mama burned hers at both ends, also in the middle too," said Laura. "Did I ever tell you really about my mama? Hell-raisingest woman in Charlotte society! North Carolina ain't forgot Mama yet. My mother was from a good family, but the family claimed she did their name no good. They put her out when I was born—I'm illegitimate, you know. The principal of the school was my father—married and a father twice before he fathered me. He never would graduate my mama from that school after she became pregnant, which he did not consider respectable for a student to do. I was born in Raleigh after all of Charlotte knew I was coming—too late for Grandpa, who was a mail carrier and a preacher, to send Mama away before the news leaked out—which is why she was always in disgrace at home. Do you think Mama cared? Never cared! She went on back to Charlotte from Raleigh and stayed right there until the day she died having her thirteenth baby at the age of forty-four. Mama should have knowed better, but she kept on producing black, yellow, and brownskin children for thirty years. Had so many marriage licenses around the house, one overlapped the other. Every time Mama got drunk, she wanted to go get married. Me, being the first one, was the only child not blessed by some kind of wedlock—Catholic, Protestant, or Justice of the Peace. I told that reporter from *Ebony* today, don't go digging too far back into my past—write about the *now,* not the *then.*"

"How come they want to write about you in the magazine?"

"Because he says you and me've got the biggest independent church in Harlem—not belonging to no denomination but our own. He asked me in what did I believe. I said, 'In myself.' Of course, I added, 'For publication, you better fix that statement up a little. Shall I grease your palm? Or do they pay you well on your magazine?' He said, 'We don't accept money from others.' So all I said was, 'Do Jesus! Have a drink.' We got on fine. Sorry you was taking your nap, Essie, when he was here interviewing. You're always resting somewhere, so you miss a lot of what's happening. But Mr. Morrison's coming back with a photographer. They gonna take pictures of our lighted cross and me in my mink coat, me in my car, me singing in the pulpit with a tambourine. Girl, our church is getting famous! Had my mama lived to see me now, she'd of forgot I was a bastard."

"Laura!"

"Well, I was—which is maybe why I'm what that *Ebony* man calls a personality—you know, like Eartha Kitt—with that little something extra on the ball. Essie, I got it from my mama. My mother could jive a man back, make him run and butt his head against the wall, lay down his month's salary at her feet, then beg her for a nickel."

"You just the other way around," yawned Essie, growing sleepy, "giving away money."

"I know. I took after my mother in reverse. Skip it! Tell a story! Mama could make a bar full of people laugh or cry, whichever way her tale went, or if it was about ghosts, scare the hell out of 'em. Mama never saw a ghost in her life, no more than I ever saw Jesus, but she could make up ghost stories to raise the hair on your head. That's where I get my gift of making up visions. I can tell 'em in church so well that even *you* believe me, Essie, and get to shouting up there in the pulpit. Sometimes, sister, I think you're real square."

"Laura, sometimes I do think you are telling the truth in the pulpit, but you just don't believe it yourself. Your experiences is stronger than your faith."

"I been through a plenty, girl, but never seen no visions. What I been through is *real*—robbed, raped, knocked down, plus being kicked on both haunches by that old Negro that bought me that new dress that time I run to you to hide. I have had experiences, Essie, not visions. High on hard likker when I was ten, converted Baptist and half drowned at baptism when I was twelve, married when I was sixteen, divorced when I was twenty, then married again by twenty-one to a simple old Negro who wanted to take care of me.

"I said, 'Baby, I can take care of myself. Don't I look like it?'

"He said, 'You're a fine figure of a woman, Laura—which is why I am willing to buy you new dishes every day just to throw at my head.' I had a temper at that time—broke two chicken platters and a gravy bowl on his bald spot. Sometimes, all of a sudden, Essie, I would coo at him real sweet—and be reaching at the same time for something to bust that man's brains out. But I hate to be kicked in the street where the lampposts is all cemented down. Otherwise, I would have picked one of them posts up and brained that joker that night I run to you. Sometimes my meanness comes out, Essie—which, I guess, is from my mother, too. My mama took a red-hot poker in Winston-Salem one night and stuck it square up a Negro's middle hole whilst he slept."

"Fatheration!" said Essie, trying to keep her eyes open.

"I admired my mother," affirmed Laura. "Sometimes I wish I had her gumption. Ball all night, play all day, drink a bootlegger dry, and still looked like a chippie when she died! Mama protected herself from all evil and got her share of life. This Haig and Haig I'm downing would be a soft drink to my mama. And that Negro Buddy—that I'm so weak about that I'm worried as to where he's at right now—to her would be nothing but a play-toy. Take Buddy serious? Not Mama! She'd bust his conk wide open. They made women in them days—and I take somewhat after her myself. But the rest of Mama's children turned out to be nothing—all fell by the wayside—except me, Sister Laura Reed. I'm a strong branch of a bitch myself."

Essie was snoring politely in a gray silk chair from Sloane's, so she made no comment. Laura poured another drink, lifted her glass, and made a toast to herself in the mirror.

"To Miss Bitch!" she said.

21

ENTER MARIETTA

When June came all over the U.S.A. and Marietta's school was out down South, it came about that at last she was coming to live in Harlem with her mother. Essie had sent her the money for two new dresses and a magic ticket North on the bus. In New York, Essie went down to the Greyhound Terminal to meet her.

Wonderland of the North—where white folks and colored folks all sit anywhere on a bus. The North where you can be colored but still get a Coca-Cola in any drugstore without having to carry it outside to drink it. The North—where young folks all go to school together. The North where New York is, Chicago, Detroit—and Harlem.

They all had come originally from the South—Essie, Laura,

Buddy, plus just about everybody else in their church, too. Mighty magnet of the colored race—the North! Roll bus! Roll across that Jim Crow River called the Potomac! Roll past the white dome of the Capitol! Roll down the New Jersey Turnpike, through the Holland Tunnel, and up and out from under the river into the North! New York! Roll into the magic streets of Manhattan! Harlem, a chocolate ice cream cone in New York's white napkin.

"Chocolate candy of a boy! Buddy, baby, daddy, do you want another little nip of Scotch now before Essie gets back here tonight with her daughter? We'd better put these drinking things away before that teenager arrives."

"I expect that kid's smelled likker before," growled Buddy.

"But I'm gonna be her 'Aunt Laura,' so no bad examples the first day."

"What are you looking at *me* for?" asked Buddy. "Do I look like a bad example?"

"Doll-baby boy," purred Laura behind the silky couch on which Buddy lounged, "lean back your head and let me kiss your sugar lips." Cool records on the victrola, rippling vibes, somebody like Milt Jackson playing "Willow, Weep For Me," cool, cool, cool, coo-ooo-oo-ol. "Baby-doll!"

"Don't call me such cute names—I'm not a poodle," growled Buddy.

Laura clawed him gently on the shoulder. "Tomcat then! Billy goat! Big black bar-stud! Mama's beautiful bastard!"

"Don't get me roused up *again* this early in the evening. Unhand me, woman!"

"You sweet old honeycomb of a joker! Tonight's Saturday—no services for me. But I'm going to bed early so's to be fresh for church tomorrow—I love that big funny old theatre we moved into!"

"You look sharp upon that stage, too, sugar—just like a grand piano, as I told you before—full front, streamlined rear."

"Soon as the backstage painting's done, I'm gonna take that big dressing room downstairs with the star on it for my robing room. Before it turned to movies, they tell me that house used to be an old vaudeville theatre. Seems like I can still smell make-up. I always did want to be in show business and have myself a dressing room."

"This church racket beats show business, baby—the way they're turning all the old theatres in Harlem into churches."

"You know what Mahalia Jackson says: 'The church will be here when the night clubs are gone.' The church is the rock. I reckon me and Essie picked a good rock on which to stand."

"That Essie's a little *too* holy and sanctified," growled Buddy. "Telling me I ought to change my ways! Kid, I've been a hustler too long now to be anything else *but*. And if it hadn't been for me, Laura, you-all Reed Sisters never would have got that old firetrap of a theatre cleared by the inspector."

The Scotch stood on the coffee table before them and now Laura was on the silky couch with Buddy.

"I'm glad you know the right people," she cooed, "in with the politicianers."

"Connections, sugar, connections! Marty can fix anything. Even in the rackets, a Negro's got to have a white man to front for him."

Laura rubbed her thumb and forefinger together indicating money. "I must say, the do-re-mi helped a little too, didn't it?"

"Greasing palms always helps, kiddo! I could do with a little change myself tonight—a few Abe Lincolns and some tens. Since you say you're going to bed early, I might take a hand of poker up at Shoofly's. How about table stakes?"

"Table stakes?"

"Say, fifty simoleons."

"Aw, honey, that's a lot of money to gamble away."

Buddy shrugged. "I can't sleep here tonight, so Essie informs me. With that young girl coming, I got to blasé my time away somewhere. Something tells me that kid's going to be in our way around here, Laura."

"Essie's daughter is no kid, Buddy. She's sixteen."

Buddy grinned. "Sweet sixteen—but I bet she's been kissed."

"Maybe not. Marietta was raised by her grandmother," said Laura, "and down South they generally raise kids right—not running wild like they do up here in Harlem. God's been good to Essie, and at last she'll have her daughter with her. I wonder if that child'll get off the bus hungry."

"I don't know about that child, but me, I could give a steak hell right now—rare, with the blood oozing out."

"They'll be here soon, then me and Essie'll fix dinner. I told her to bring in some groceries. Meanwhile I better get decent and put on a dress, heh? Also let's put this likker away *right now,* and rinse out the glasses. You do it, Daddy, while I get pretty. Be sweet."

"O. K.," said Buddy, "go ahead and make like Lena Horne."

Laura went down the hall to her room and Buddy took a couple straight before he put the House of Lords away in a built-in cabinet in the wall opposite the lighted panel of a cross. When all the other lights were out in the living room, the cross glowed softly. Above it was Essie's motto: GOD BLESS THIS HOME.

That must be her now putting a key in the lock. It was. And behind Essie, came Marietta. When Buddy looked up, in the door there stood a tiny, a well-formed, a golden-skinned, a delicate-featured, a doll-handed, a pretty-as-a-picture, a blossoming peaches-and-cream of a girl.

"Why, good evening! I didn't know you'd still be here, Buddy," Essie said. "Marietta, meet Mr. Lomax. Mr. Lomax, my daughter."

Buddy stood up. Slowly his lighthouse smile spread. Then softly he took the young girl's hand. "Pleased to know you, Marietta. Essie, you got a bee-ooo-tiful daughter!"

Marietta's eyes were big as saucers, almost as big as Buddy's. When he finally dropped her hand, she cried, "Mama, it's so pretty in here! Oh, Mama, what a nice place you've got—so modernistic! And a lighted cross in the wall!"

"We're blessed, honey! But just wait until you see our new church tomorrow. All of this is the Lord's own miracle, Marietta. But where is Laura?" Essie called, "Laura, Laura!"

"I'm coming, coming," strong voice from down the hall. Then cool in her summer frock, Laura came, arms out to Marietta. "Child, I'm your Aunt Laura."

"This is my old friend who's stuck by me through thick and thin," said Essie. "This is Laura."

"I'm glad you're here, Marietta! This is your house." Laura took her in her arms.

"I wish *I* was related, too," grinned Buddy. But Essie didn't hear him.

"Thank God! I just thank God for all," Essie said glowing.

"God—and your tambourines," laughed Buddy. "Marietta, can you play a tambourine?"

Shyly, "I used to try sometimes in church down home."

"Then you'll fit," said Buddy.

"Are you part of the choir at the church?" asked Marietta.

"No, baby," he said, "I'm just a backstage man."

"Buddy," Laura's tone was sharp, "her name's Marietta, not *baby*."

"She's a baby to me," said Buddy. "And I'm sure glad you got here, little old gal, so we can have dinner."

"Oh, my goodness!" Essie exclaimed. "Meeting Marietta, I was so excited I clean forgot to bring the chops. Ain't that awful!"

"No," said Buddy, "not so bad—because my mouth's set on steaks anyhow, so I'll go get 'em. Um-m-m—with the blood oozing out! Come on, Marietta, lemme show you where the stores are in this neighborhood, since you'll be living here. We'll get some sirloins, ice cream, and beer. What else do you need, Laura?"

"Potatoes," said Laura drily, as her eyes narrowed.

"Marietta, ain't you kinder tired?" asked Essie.

"Not really, Mama."

"Oh, let the girl see what our block looks like—take a little squint at Harlem," said Buddy. "Come on, kid."

Marietta looked at Essie eagerly. "All right, Mama?"

"You-all come directly back then," said Essie weakly, "and while you're gone we'll set the table."

Had Laura said anything at all then, she would have screamed. As soon as the door closed, she went to the cabinet and got a drink. "I'll steal one while your child's out," she said, "so she won't think right off the bat that I'm a likker-head." Then she turned and smiled at Essie. "She's a mighty pretty girl, Essie— I'm afraid too pretty for this city of sin. Don't you think maybe

Marietta should just stay here for a *little* visit, then go on back to her grandma down in the simple old South?"

"After all these years," said Essie, "I want to keep my child with me."

"She's at the age, you know—" warned Laura.

"Well, there's some mighty nice young mens in Harlem—in our church," Essie said. "I already told young C.J. my daughter was coming, and to drop around tonight."

"Oh, God, I hope C.J. don't bring that guitar of his! The last thing I want to hear is gospel music on my night off. I be's good all the week in front of the public, *plus on Sunday*. But on Saturday night I feel like letting my hair down."

"I hope you won't drink so much, now that Marietta is here."

"I'll do my damndest to respect your child, Essie, I swear I will. But you know I ain't no saint. You've just naturally got goodness in you. Long as I've known you, you never was inclined to do nothing much—but set on your big fat behind and let the city pay your rent. Me, I'm active. But you, you just take whatever comes. Thank God, for all our sakes, it's money coming these days."

"I wrestles with temptation, too, Laura, in my heart. But somehow or another, I always did want to *try* to be good. Once I thought—just like you said about me—being good was doing nothing, I guess, so I done nothing for half my life. Now, I'm trying to do *something*—and be good, too. That's harder. It's easy to preach holy, but hard to live holy."

"You're reading a mighty lot lately"—Laura pointed to the pile of books on the table—"which is strangely for you, who never even read the Bible till we started this church. Now you're *buying* books."

"Just Thurman, and Reverend Robinson and Norman Vincent Peale. I want to see what them men say about being good."

"I don't trust nothing white folks write, especially about being good, the way they behave down South."

"Howard Thurman ain't white. He's a colored preacher. So's Reverend Robinson. As for that Mr. Peale, I'm no respecter of race, Laura. Some white folks is good, some bad, just like the rest of us. What I'm trying to do, now that I've got the time—"

"And money," interrupted Laura.

"And money to set down and meditate, is to try to unscramble the good from the bad—in myself and others. If I can just separate the good in this world, the wheat from the tares, maybe I can hold onto it. I found a verse in the Bible I been studying over and over, says, 'Canst thou by searching find out God?' "

"What verse is that?" asked Laura sitting up straight. "Where is it?"

"Job 11-7."

"What a number!" cried Laura. "11-7, wow! 7-11."

"Laura, you thinking about the numbers, and I'm thinking about finding God—finding out what *is* God in terms of what we is—us, you and me—on this earth. Reverend Thurman says—"

"Reverend Thurman don't know no more than you do about God. He ain't nothing but a man, and we're all made in God's image, both men and women. I'm gonna try to stay as good-looking as I can myself. It takes money to go to Rose Meta's—which is one more *fine* beauty shop—but I intend to go every week."

"It takes money to run a good church, too. And now that we got a big place, Laura, I wants me a day nursery in the basement of our church where mothers what goes to work can leave their children and—oh, sister, there's so many ways to do good and *be* good that we ain't found yet."

"Listen, Essie, *how* good do you want to be—so good you ain't got a dime? I'm trying to figure out how we can make *plenty* of money. My mink coat's costing me Three Thousand Dollars! And now you got a daughter here in New York to educate. Takes money to put a young girl through school right."

"I wants other people's daughters to get through school too. There ain't no being good and keeping goodness to yourself. Is there, Laura?"

"It's good to me when it's just *all* mine, Essie. It's like love— like Buddy. I don't want to share Buddy with nobody."

"You talking about flesh-kind of love, not spirit."

"The spirit works in mysterious ways. When I open my mouth to sing, it feels just like when I open it for a kiss—*so good*, like being in bed with Buddy."

"Laura!"

"Well it does—same kind of thrill—especially when I hit them high notes in swing time. Ow! But by the way, I wonder where is Buddy?"

22

STEAK FOR DINNER

The bell rang, but it was C.J. at the door, and he *did* have his guitar. Essie made him welcome, for C.J. was one of the nice young men in their gospel choir, or rather in the singing band at one side of the rostrum that accompanied the choir. There Birdie Lee had set up her drums along with the guitar, trumpet, and an old man who blowed on a flute, while the two pianos at either side of the stage sometimes drowned them all out, except the drums. Nobody could top Birdie Lee when her sticks really got going.

C.J. played a nice gospel guitar. "And I'm working on some brand-new spiritual riffs out of this world, Sister Essie, for that new song the Tambourine Chorus is trying out tomorrow night."

"Some saints can overdo, C.J.," said Laura, leaving for the

kitchen to start the coffee boiling. "You just set down and rest yourself. Put your gitfiddle in the corner. You can serenade the young lady when she comes."

"Bless God, son, you do play pretty!"

"Does your daughter sing?" C.J. asked Essie.

"To tell the truth, I don't know, C.J., but I hope she do. You ask her."

"I will," said C.J. "Where's she at?"

"She'll be here directly."

Sure enough, directly Marietta and Buddy arrived loaded down with things to eat and drink, including Buddy's carrying a dozen cans of beer, three of which he promptly opened, handing one to C.J. and offering another to Marietta. But she declined. C.J. demurred, saying he did not drink beer. But Buddy made him feel like less than a man if he couldn't drink that weak stuff. No kid likes to be made out a sissy in front of a pretty girl, even if he is a junior saint, so C.J. drank the beer, and shortly felt it. Meanwhile, in spite of Buddy, he got acquainted with Marietta.

"That's a pretty name."

"And yours," asked Marietta, "what really is your first name?"

"My first name's just C.J."

"What does C.J. stand for?"

"C.J., that's all," said the young man. "I only got initials for a first name."

But Buddy cut in, "Christ Jesus, baby, Christ Jesus, that's what it stands for."

"Mr. Lomax is just kidding, Marietta," said C.J.

"C.J. is one of them holy and sanctified boys," said Buddy.

"I was raised up in a gospel church, but—"

"Probably won't even take a chick to the movies."

"Sure I will," bristled C.J.

"Never see you around the pool halls," insisted Buddy.

"Well, with school work and all—"

"Where do you go to school, C.J.?" asked Marietta.

"First year college at City," said C.J.

"Can I look at your guitar, kid?" asked Buddy. "I used to beat out a mean blues before I left Savannah."

"A blues? Sure, if the Sisters don't mind."

"A little blues won't hurt the Sisters. Hum-mm! You got a nice box here."

"I play in the college orchestra sometimes."

"You're lucky to be in college," said Marietta.

"My Korean GI money," said C.J.

"What are you taking up?"

"Chemistry. I can analyze that Holy Water Sister Laura dispenses in church. I wish she'd let me test a bottle while I'm here tonight, so I can tell what makes Jordan Water different from that we have in New York City."

"That Jordan Water costs a dollar a bottle, boy," drawled Buddy, "so nobody's giving none away."

"Well, maybe I'll buy a bottle at church tomorrow."

"I would advise you to leave that water alone," said Buddy.

"Why?" asked C.J., puzzled.

"Just advice, that's all," said Buddy as the first eight bars of a down-home stomp rolled off the guitar strings. "How do you like my blues, boy?"

"Right nice, Mr. Lomax. Marietta, whereabouts are you in school—high, or what?"

"Second year high school. But you know the schools down

South aren't very good, especially for colored, and—" She was speaking louder and louder as Buddy's blues mounted, too. "Well, I'm afraid I won't match the girls up North here."

"You look real smart to me, Marietta. Besides, you're so pretty you scare me." But the boy had to shout his last few words. Buddy was drowning them out with the blues, sniffing at the same time at the scent of food from the back of the house.

Apron on from the kitchen, Essie put a stop to it. "I knowed that couldn't be C.J. playing that loud. Buddy, the neighbors! They'll hear all them blues coming out of our apartment and think we've forgot the gospel."

With a belly chord, Buddy tossed the guitar to C.J. "Here, kid, you can play the kind of stuff the Sisters like. But them gospel songs sound just like blues to me."

"Buddy! At least our words is different. But we don't need no music now, boys, nohow. We're about to put the steaks on the fire. Anybody want to wash up for dinner?"

"I'm a clean boy myself, thanks," said Buddy.

But C.J. spoke up. "I do, Sister Essie."

"I'll show you the place," said Essie, "and when you've washed your hands, son, come on out in the kitchen and cut the watermelon. Dinner'll soon be ready." C.J. followed Essie down the hall.

"He's country," said Buddy, with a head-down smile. He was looking at Marietta. "Baby, I'd like to show you something."

"On the guitar?" asked Marietta.

"No, not on the guitar."

"What?" He was very near her now.

"You've only met two men in New York so far."

"Why, I've only been here an—"

"I know. You met *me* first," said Buddy. "It's up to me to school you."

"School me?"

"That's right. That gospel boy of a C.J. ain't dry behind the ears yet. Men don't start asking a sharp little chick like you what school you're in."

"Sharp?"

"Stacked, solid, neat-all-reet, copasetic, baby!"

"Thank you, Mr. Buddy."

"Don't *Mister* Buddy me. Just call me Buddy, that's all—Big-Eyed Buddy—with eyes for you."

"Mama told me you're Miss Laura's friend."

"Marietta, Laura is as old as your mama—and I'm mighty near as young as you."

"Still and yet, you're her friend, aren't you?"

"I'm her friend. But, Marietta, I'm gonna show you something. I'm gonna show you how fast a real Harlem stud moves in."

"Moves in?"

"On a chick." Before she could pass, Buddy's arm swept her to him. His body was warm. The old symbol of the earth suddenly sounded as if beaten by the sun in the first Garden. "We start like this," he breathed. Buddy kissed her.

"You told me you liked your steaks rare—with the blood oozing out," said Laura very quietly from the doorway. She had come to call them to dinner.

Before Marietta could struggle free, he dropped his arms. "I do," Buddy said.

"And your women tender?"

"Could be," said Buddy.

"You, Miss Marietta, I guess you're not as innocent as you look."

"I tried to get past, Aunt Laura, but—"

"Then get past, honey, *get past quick!* As for you, Buddy-boy—"

"Aw, come, old chick, don't get blood in your eyes."

"Nor on my hands?" asked Laura. "I never knowed a Negro yet that didn't bleed—if cut."

Essie's voice rang out in the hall. "Let's go, everybody, dinner!"

"Come on, Buddy, get your steak," said Laura.

23

LUCKY TEXTS

After Marietta came, Laura didn't bring Buddy home so often. After services they went elsewhere in Laura's car. The big new apartment was quiet, and Essie had a chance to get acquainted with her daughter. Only C.J. was there sometimes, properly courting the kid. Essie liked C.J. for he was a clean, quiet gospel boy, bright and not bad-looking. Marietta liked him, too. But even when he held her tightly in his arms on the silky couch, nothing electric happened as had happened that one and only time when Buddy moved in behind the magnet of his chocolate shadow. About that, no one said a thing to Essie—not Laura, Buddy, or Marietta. Now Marietta avoided Buddy.

The Tambourine Choir filled the new church with music, and

Marietta became a part of the singing. When her mother introduced her to the congregation she had, all alone, begun a chorus of "Rise and Shine and Give God the Glory." All the instruments and voices had supported her and the whole church sang too, along with the singing in Essie's heart that her daughter had come to her at last. That night, taking advantage of the wave of wonder in the church, Laura chose to introduce the Lucky Texts of which Essie had no inkling. As Marietta took her seat in the banked choir loft and the singing died down and Essie sat fanning in her big red chair, Laura stepped forward and thanked God for Essie, Marietta, and the Tambourine Chorus.

"And now," she said, "I've got something new for you, church. After this fine chorus that you are going to hear on the air waves of the nation soon, and before I introduce our up-and-coming TV quartet, the Gloriettas, I got a surprise for everybody, right out of the Book—the Bible. And not one, but four surprises. I am going to give you four texts for the week—Lucky Texts, picked out with prayer and meditation on my part from the Holy Book. For each Lucky Text, members and friends, I want you to drop a quarter—or a dollar for all four—in the tambourines as they pass. Girls of the Offeratory, circulate amongst the congregation for their free-will gifts."

Essie leaned forward. "Laura, you gonna stop the services to take up a collection now?"

"I am," whispered Laura. "This is a special collection, so just hold your horses, Essie."

She turned again to the people, opened the big Bible on the rostrum and fingered its gilt-edged pages.

"Friends, I want you-all to write down the numbers of these

Lucky Texts, and study these texts all during the week—until I give out some more next Sunday. Get your quarters ready, your dollar bills, and your pencils. Now write."

Laura pretended to look at the Bible, wetting her thumb to turn its pages, but what she really looked at was a slip of paper she had lying on the rostrum.

"Psalms 9 and 20," she said. "Got that? 9 and 20. Now drop a quarter in the tambourines. For each text a quarter. Give God His, folks, and you'll get yours! . . . Next text: Leviticus 2-16, Chapter 2, verse 16. Take down all three numbers: 2-1-6. Twenty-five cents. You'll have no luck if you don't give God His'n. 2-16, yes! Aw, let 'em clink! Let the holy coins clink! . . . Now, again, ready? Revelations 12-3. Got it? 12-3. Let me read that text to you. Listen: 'And there appeared another wonder in heaven; and behold a great red dragon, having seven heads and ten horns, and seven crowns upon his heads.' What a text! What a mighty text! Revelations 12-3! Yes, one-two-three! And in the text itself, *seven* heads and *ten* horns—the number *seven* and the number *ten*. Look up this text yourself— Revelations 12-3. . . . And now the last one. Oh, what a great text, too—Sister Essie's favorite! But I ain't gonna tell you what this one is. Just write the number on your pads, then look it up yourself. Read it and see for yourself. So take the numbers down—Job 11-7. Carefully, now! Write it right—Job 11-7. I said 7, 7-11, or 11-7 either way. Yes, bless God, children! 11-7, that's right. Job 11-7."

The rhythm of Laura's phrases and the magic of the numbers, the 3, the 11, and the 7 to top them all, caused many among the crowd to cry aloud "Thank you, Sister Laura! Thank you!

Thanks, thanks! Thank you!" The tambourines were filled with money when the ushers returned to the rostrum. Laura estimated two, maybe three hundred dollars.

"There'll be some numbers played tomorrow," Buddy could not resist crying from his third-row seat.

Essie said, "Just listen at that Buddy taking everything wrong."

Laura said, "Amen!" as if she had not heard. "Now a little holy music. Let me introduce to you for another happy time our singing pride, our Temple's fine young women, the Four Gloriettas."

The two gleaming grand pianos trilled, C.J.'s guitar joined the pianos, Birdie's drums rolled, the trumpet played a golden note, and four buxom girls came forward shod in golden slippers and mauve robes to sing a song about the glory of touching God's garment that ended:

> *"There will be a shower of stars!*
> *There will be a blaze of light!*
> *All around my Saviour's head*
> *A diadem so bright!*
> *You will see it from afar*
> *As you stand beside His throne.*
> *Oh, when you touch His garment*
> *He will claim you for His own!"*

For many there living in the tenements of Harlem, to believe in such wonder was worth every penny the tambourines collected.

24

SET TO ASCEND

"Seventeen converts last night, including the man with one eye and one arm. This church is growing, Essie. But big as it is, it's already busting at the seams."

In the big room under the stage of Tambourine Temple as the midweek preliminary song service drew toward its close, with the choir singing upstairs, Laura and Essie were robing to make their entrance. As usual Laura was talking.

"Since I gave Buddy that red car for his birthday, Essie, I've been having to drive myself—or else get a chauffeur. So what do you think? I'm gonna *get* a chauffeur."

"Ostentation is a sin, Laura."

"So's having too much money, according to you. But there's

nothing I love as much as *too* much money. And the way it's pouring in every night upstairs, I'm gonna stack up loot on the living room table next year and stare at it."

"Laura!"

"You can buy anything with money, honey, which is why I love it."

"Sister, darling, I hope you won't mind what I say—but don't you think maybe money can do harm sometimes? I hope you ain't spoiling yourself—and Buddy."

"Do I mingle and meddle in your affairs, Essie?"

"I wouldn't say nothing if you wasn't my friend."

"Sometimes friendship can rile even a friend, Sister. Just look out for yourself and your little girl, and I'll look out for me, see! And whilst I'm on the subject of Marietta, maybe you ought to send her back down South—or else move to the suburbs, one."

"Thanks for the hint, Laura. I reckon you feel crowded, now that Marietta's come. I didn't want to leave you—unless you told me to."

"Girl, you ain't Ruth, and I ain't Naomi. And you got your daughter's morals to protect. They call this thing a tiara," murmured Laura, putting on her head a gold band with a cross in front. "Goes nice with this robe, don't it, Essie?"

"Um-humm!" said Essie. "But I wonder what is Marietta and C.J. doing outside in the door so long. Why don't them kids come on in here?"

"Necking," said Laura. "I hope you don't think C.J. really is named after Christ, do you?"

"Aw, now, Laura, them children—"

"Children, my eye!"

"I got shoes, you got shoes
All of God's chillun got shoes!
When I get to heaven
Gonna put on my shoes!
Gonna walk all over God's heaven . . ."

Laura took a few syncopated steps to the music rollicking down from above.

"Heaven! Heaven!
Everybody talks about
Heaven ain't going there . . ."

"Just listen at that fine singing upstairs, girl!" Laura cried. "We got some good gospel musicianers, I mean!"

"You really organized a fine band, Laura. You're the backbone of it all."

"Entertain people at Tambourine Temple, that's what I say. You sing and pray, Sister, and I will arrange the show."

"It's more than a show, Laura. You've done better than you know—God is in this church."

"I still got feet of clay, Essie. You're the soul. But please powder your face a little before you go upstairs. That spotlight on the rostrum shows up your liver spots."

Laura handed Essie her compact. While she stood in front of the mirror, Marietta and C.J. came running in.

"Mama," panted Marietta, "C.J. wants to know can he take me out for a hamburger tonight after services?"

"I'll bring her right home," swore C.J.

"Not to your home—*ours*, I hope," said Laura.

"Yes'm, Sister Laura."

"I guess it's all right, son, if she wants to go," said Essie. "But behave your-all's selves."

"That's settled," said Laura, "so get on up with the band, C.J., where you should've been. Marietta, you hear that Tambourine Chorus shaking, don't you?"

"Yes, Aunt Laura," said Marietta getting her robe from the closet.

"Tell them musicianers, C.J., to give me and Essie a lot of noise when we appear on the stage—rostrum, I mean. I want plenty of *Thank Gods* tonight, honey, bass chords, drum rolls, tambourines, and hallelujahs from all of you-all."

"Yes, ma'am!" answered C.J., as he and Marietta ran up the stairs to the rostrum.

"The Spirit don't need all that ballyhoo and theatre kind of build-up," murmured Essie.

"No, baby, but Laura Reed does. Are you all set to ascend the pulpit?"

"I'm set to ascend."

"Now, I wonder how come them drums upstairs stop playing just when I'm ready to appear?" growled Laura.

"You know Sister Birdie Lee's weakness," Essie said. "I bet she's heading down here."

"That little old hussy we picked up in the gutter can really beat some drums," admitted Laura, "even if she is kinder hateful."

Essie was right. Birdie Lee came scooting down the stairs. "Excuse me, you-all, but I drunk so much beer when I was a sinner that I'm still going to the Ladies' Room. Excuse me!"

"Hurry up, sister, and pee," said Laura, "so you can roll them drums when I step on the stage. Come on, Essie, we'll wait upstairs for Birdie to return. I like plenty of noise when I mount the rostrum. You can sneak in the pulpit quiet if you want to, but I want the world to know when Sister Laura Reed arrives. Let's we ascend."

25

ONE LOST LAMB

To make his conversion believable, Laura felt, it would have to be worked out carefully, and fortunately she had a flair for such things. The hymn she chose for Buddy's cue to salvation was "The Ninety and Nine." With her pianists, Laura rehearsed it several times.

"You're around the church so much these days, officiating and helping me," said Laura to Buddy as they drove through Central Park one afternoon, "that lots of saints are wondering how come you don't belong to our church—how come you're not converted?"

"So it would be good business then if I came into the fold, huh?"

"It would cover little Mama," said Laura, "and I wouldn't have to answer so many questions."

"Since nothing exciting ever happens in the middle of the week, suppose I get converted Wednesday," said Buddy, curving past the Tavern on the Green.

"Fine!" cried Laura. "That might cool Essie down a little. But listen, Daddy, after you get converted, don't go getting *too* holy. Just learn to melt a little more. Be a little nicer to me, and don't be so hard."

"Don't *don't* me, sugar," barked Buddy, stopping for a red light, then playfully ramming a fist under Laura's chin. "I know how far to go, up or down, right, left, or in between."

"Which is what I like about you," murmured Laura. "Baby, you dig the angles."

"All the angles." Buddy flashed his lighthouse smile as their car purred away.

"There were ninety and nine that safely lay
In the shelter of the fold . . ."

Laura never looked prettier nor sang better than she did that Wednesday night as the services drew near the close. Her tambourine lay silent on the altar. Only the two pianos played softly, very softly, behind her. Laura had expressly commanded Birdie Lee *not* to hit a tap as she sang. "And *don't* sing with me!" The orchestra was not to play, only the soft, soft, sad, sweet pianos. There were almost a thousand people in the church, but Laura was singing to Buddy. The congregation knew only that she had asked for converts, requesting all who wanted to come to God to walk down the aisle and accept salvation.

Laura had not intended to cry on the rostrum. But as she sang, somehow in spite of herself, tears came. She found herself suddenly wishing that she, too, were like Essie seated in the red chair behind her—truly a Christian.

> "One lamb was out in the hills away
> Far from the gates of gold . . ."

Lamb! Buddy! Buddy! Tower-tall Buddy! Unsaved Buddy!

> "Away on the mountain wild and bare,
> Away from the tender Shepherd's care."

How lonely the song, how lost and lonely, as Laura turned and walked toward the rostrum where the Bernstein Bible shone.

Sobs broke out in the old rat-trap of a theatre-church and Deacon Crow-For-Day cried, "I once stood in the wilderness, too. I were lost! I were lost!" Laura pointed to the massed choir on the platform in their singing robes.

> "Lord, Thou hast here Thy ninety and nine:
> Are they not enough for Thee?
> But the Shepherd made answer,
> One of mine has wandered away from me.
> Although the road be rough and steep,
> I go to the desert to find my sheep,
> I go to the desert to find my sheep."

A piercing cry rent the auditorium and a woman fainted. Laura looked down at the long aisle that ran through the auditorium to the vestibule and out to the hard road of the Harlem pavements and she saw the park where the taxis sped up from Penn Station where the trains came in from the South where the roads were unpaved and the shacks had no windowpanes and the money for the ticket North had been purchased with sweat, maybe blood, and sin, and surely sorrow:

> "Lord, whose are those blood drops all the way
> That mark out the mountain's track?
> They were shed for one who had gone astray
> Ere the Shepherd could bring him back.
> Lord, whence are Thy hands so rent and torn?"

How could Laura's hands be the Lord's uplifted there? But somehow they were His hands when she lifted them up. Nobody doubted that those hands were the Lord's hands.

> "They are pierced tonight by many a thorn,
> Yes, pierced tonight by many a thorn."

Look! Look! My hands! My dark hands! Shaking the brooms and mops of a nation, scrubbing and cleaning the floors of a nation, mining the coal of a nation, carting the slag of a nation, cleaning the outhouses of a nation.

> "But none of the ransomed ever knew
> How deep were the waters crossed,
> How dark was the night
> That the Lord passed through
> Ere He found His sheep that was lost."

So lone! So lost!

*"Out in the desert He heard its cry,
So lone, so helpless, ready to die."*

"Save me! Lord save me," cried Buddy.

Buddy was not sure himself then that he did not mean his cry. Suddenly he got up and stumbled to the altar. Then the drums rolled—for Birdie Lee forgot what she had been told. The old man played on his flute, the trumpet blew a golden note, C.J.'s guitar sounded like a thousand strings, the tempo changed and Laura's voice hit each word hard like a trip hammer:

*"All through the mountains thunder-riven
And up from the rocky steep,
Oh, there arose a glad cry to the gates of heaven,
Rejoice! I have found my sheep!"*

Then the chorus picked up the words and a hundred voices proclaimed:

"God has found, God has found His sheep."

So it was that Big-Eyed Buddy became a member of Tambourine Temple. And at that moment nobody doubted Buddy's conversion except Essie, who seldom in all her life had taken the Lord's name in vain. But when she saw Buddy bow at Laura's feet to beat his head upon the floor crying, "I'm saved! I'm saved! Thank God, I'm saved!" Essie said, "This is the Goddamndest shame yet!"

She then went into a pause from which nothing could move her until everybody had gone home. Then she put out the lights in the empty theatre and locked the door.

26

MOON OVER HARLEM

Big moon, golden moon, sifting its rays down through the trees in the park.

"You asked me to tell you about my mother, C.J.," said Marietta, "so, even if you have got something else on your mind, *I'm going to tell you about my mother*. Listen!"

C.J. held her close, very close in his arms on the park bench.

"I know Sister Essie's a good woman, Marietta, so there's not much more to tell, is there?"

"She *is* a good woman. Like I told you, Mama wanted me to be with her for years, but she couldn't manage it. She didn't just want me to be with her under any kind of circumstances. I wanted to be, though, but she didn't. Mama wanted things nice for me—a big apartment and all—and she waited until they were nice."

"Nice," C.J. said, his hand following the warm curve of her breast.

"C.J., I know you're the same way—I can tell you're good. And, listen! If you want to make love to me now—the way you want to right now, here in this park in the dark—if you was to have me now, then you wouldn't want me maybe when things got right for us."

"I would, I would want you," whispered C.J., "I would."

"Maybe you'd want me, but you'd think you shouldn't."

"I'd want you! I want you *now*, and I'd want you any time, all the time."

"You might disrespect me, C.J., if I gave in to you *quick* like this. We've only known each other a little short while. I love you, C.J., but I want you to love me, too, not just—be with me."

"I got to be with you, Marietta, I got to, I need to."

"You will, sweetest boy in the world, you will—but please, not tonight."

"Suntanned, honey-brown, honey-gold, you're sweet, you're sweet! You're so sweet!"

"No, C.J."

Suddenly he was angry. "Aw, you ain't all that pure." He took his arms away and put his hands into his pockets. Silence. Moonlight. Leaves.

"I'm not pretending to anything, C.J.—except I love you, that's all."

"You love me?" said C.J., as if he'd never heard the word before. "You really love me?"

"I love you."

"I love you, too, Marietta. I'll be damned if I (pardon me, I'm a saint) I'll be *dogged* if I don't! Come on! I'll walk you home."

He didn't touch her any more. He just looked at her in the soft drift of moonlight that came through the trees. Then C.J. stood up. Obediently, Marietta rose from the park bench and took his hand.

"If that Buddy guy, or anybody else, tries to touch you in New York City, or anywhere else, I'll beat the living be-Jesus out of 'em."

"Kiss me."

"Marietta!"

27

SHOWER

The nights when Buddy stayed with Laura, in the morning he would take a shower and when he took a shower, to Laura Buddy was like iron walking through the room naked to the shower, as clean and hard before the water fell as afterwards, glistening clean.

When Laura took a shower and walked around the room naked, to Buddy she was like chocolate in summer on the verge of going soft, yal, about to become sticky, melt, before or after the water fell the same.

About Buddy nothing at all sweet-sticky to Laura. Nothing about Laura firm and unsticky to Buddy, body soft and gooey like chocolate over almonds in a summer almond bar. A too-sweet taste in the mind's mouth, yal, too much.

To Laura no taste at all—the hard clean iron of tall brown glistening Buddy. Cool smooth nothing-to-rub-off, to skin like fruit, nothing to bite off, keep, dry like a flower in a book, smell, taste about Buddy, nothing.

Everything melting, to need-to-wipe-your-fingers-clean, sweet sticky softness about Laura, even after a cold shower. The smell of woman, even after a shower. Like it? Sure, yal! Love it? Naw! I get sick to my stomach.

"I need ten dollars for a couple of Scotches, baby, on my way to church. I said ten dollars, Laura!"

Buddy, don't you ever, Buddy, Buddy, ever need to just hold, need to hold me, Buddy, hold me still and quiet still-like, do nothing but hold me? I am Laura! How can you be so big, organ-sounding words, brown, strong, straight, clean, big—and nothing gives at all, bends, melts to me, warms me in my heart at all? So damned-looking clean—iron legs, thighs, iron chest, iron arms, hard, hard iron lips, teeth, iron tongue—nothing gives. In the end nothing. I try to imagine, Buddy, I try.

"Throw me a towel—two towels—two big towels, baby."

"I can't hear you, Buddy, with the water running."

"You *better* hear me, Laura, and throw me a towel!"

"Buddy . . ."

28

CROSS TO BEAR

Meanwhile, that summer Essie moved to Mount Vernon, made the down payment on a little frame house there—a house with a front porch and a back porch and in the yard an old-fashioned rocking two-seated wooden swing that the former tenant left behind. She and Marietta loved it. They could sit outdoors all the afternoon in the back yard rocking, have a dog, a cat, canary birds, and Essie could go barefooted around the house again as she used to do down South, and fill the icebox with soft drinks and watermelon and forget the smell of wine and whiskey. Somehow she didn't miss Laura. They saw each other every night but Saturday at the church. Essie became a commuter, up and down the steps of the 125th Street Station, from Harlem to the suburbs and back by train.

What He's done for me!
What He's done for me!
I never shall forget
What He's done for me!

Now Laura had the fine apartment all to herself, which was just what Laura wished—except that she did miss Essie. And Buddy—whose birthday present had been the red car—didn't stay there as much any more, now that he could stay freely. Just like a tomcat of a man! To Laura's ears in the beauty shop came rumors, and the rumors turned out to be true. One day on Seventh Avenue Laura saw her with her own eyes sitting in the sleek new Cadillac with the top down and Buddy at the wheel. She had the kind of hair that blew in her eyes—this other woman—and was as young as Marietta.

"Jesus had a cross to bear, so has everyone," quoted the beauty shop operator who served Laura, of course to another customer. "But that pretty little model's a glamorous cross for Laura Reed to have to put up with—after all that money she's spent on that Negro Buddy. A no-good dog!"

"Them handsome dogs is the worst kind," said the customer. "I would not have no handsome man for mine, with all the women in town eying him. No, sir, not Claybelle Jones."

"Miss Jones, nor would I," said the beauty shop operator. "And if I did, I wouldn't give him a thing but my money, not my heart. But that sanctified Reed sister loves that devil. I can feel the fever in her brow since he's started acting up. I see her temples throbbing whilst I am fixing her hair. Laura's going to have nervous prostitution if she don't watch out. And all over Buddy Lomax, who everybody knows is a mother-fouler."

"A good-looking rounder!"

"The Bible says, 'As an eagle fouleth his nest!' Miss Jones, how wide do you want this blond streak I'm putting in your hair?"

"Same width as from the left eyebrow to my right," said Claybelle Jones. "Just a little blond ripple to tease the men."

"Sister Essie's got sense. She's buying herself a home in the country."

"So I heard."

"And educating her daughter."

"Pretty as Dorothy Dandridge."

"They tell me that's what started it all—Buddy tried to make Marietta."

"Which is why Essie picked up her bed and walked to Westchester. I wish Buddy would try to make me. I'd give him at least a jigger of a break."

"Buddy's a keen-looking stud."

"Heartbreaker! That Big-Eyed Buddy!"

"A cross for any woman to bear."

"Yes, Jesus, Lord!"

"Now, girl, look in the mirror. How do you like your new hair style?"

"Solid, honey, solid! That's boss!"

29

APPLE OF EVIL

When in the dusk-dark of evening Laura's big black Cadillac drew up to the stage door of the Temple and her new little old black chauffeur jumped spryly out to open the door for her, Laura could hear inside the Tambourine Chorus:

"Listen to the lambs all a-cryin' . . .*"*

It sounded beautiful indeed. But since Laura did not see Buddy's car parked anywhere in the street, there was a frown on her face as she went inside and down the corridor to the big room under the stage. Upstairs the evening song service had started.

"Listen to the lambs all a-cryin'—
I want to go to heaven when I die."

The big room was empty save for Sister Mattie Morningside, the Mistress of the Robes, a title lately given that large and amiable woman who was Laura's personal saint, attendant, and caretaker of her churchly garments. She was always downstairs faithfully awaiting Laura's arrival every night.

"Evening, Sister Morningside! Ain't Sister Essie here yet?"

"No, Sister Laura. You know, since she's moved, it takes her a right smart time to get down here from the country."

"Seems so. And Brother Buddy?"

"Not yet, neither. But the chorus is all upstairs, singing wonderful. That's Sister Birdie Lee now."

"Set down! Well, I can't set down!
I just got to heaven and I can't set down!"

"I hear her," muttered Laura, "attracting attention to herself. Hang my coat up carefully on a hanger in the closet—and *lock* the closet. Minks don't grow on trees, Sister Mattie."

"Sure don't—and you got a *fine* piece of skin here for a lady minister."

"Since prostitutes dress good, and call girls and madams, there's no reason why saints shouldn't."

"Saints should look the best," said Sister Mattie as she disappeared into the anteroom. While Laura was taking the heavy costume jewelry off her arms, Buddy came in and threw his camel's hair coat over the table.

"So you beat me here tonight, heh, babes? My little red convertible can't purr like your big old car, I guess."

"You're kinder late."

"I started from the apartment just after you did."

"No stops on the way?"

"Just a nip at the Shalimar."

"Well, nip yourself on up the steps with some cases of that Holy Water for the congregation tonight."

"Hell, Laura, why didn't you let your driver pack them cases up?"

"He's a chauffeur, not a saint—paid to *drive*. But you're a part of this church now since your conversion."

"You can't say good ain't happening. Marty's grinning like a chesscat over the way his number writers have been picking up business since you been giving out them Lucky Texts—eighteen thousand dollars in this neighborhood last week."

"That ofay gangster ought to be happy."

"Laura, if you don't tell nobody, I'll let you in on a secret. Marty's gonna give you a diamond wrist watch for Christmas."

"I can sport it, too, baby."

"Marty asked me what should he give Sister Essie, but I told him to leave her be, *period*! Just don't give her nothing—and start that old hassle over right and wrong again. Seems like Essie even yet don't think *I'm* converted."

"You ain't—and I'm glad she moved that daughter of hers out of your path."

"Marietta's squab for C.J., I guess. But *you're* pig-meat for me." And he ran one hand down the neck of Laura's dress. But Laura drew back.

"Sometimes, Buddy, I'm disgusted with everything about you—but you."

He laughed. "Cut the kidding, Laura! It's hot down here. I'm gonna pack a case of Jordan Water upstairs and stand in the wings and listen to your rock and roll. Are you coming up?"

"I'll be up directly. Looks like a big crowd, so I got to robe myself sweet tonight. Believe I'll wear the scarlet with the gold stole."

"Gild your lily," said Buddy. "Decorate your righteous hide!" He disappeared into the corridor and up the iron steps to the stage with a case of Jordan Water on his shoulder, so Sister Mattie knew it was time for her to come back with the robes. She brought three of various colors for Laura's selection.

"The scarlet one tonight," said Laura, "maybe the Nile green tomorrow."

Upstairs the music mounted and Laura knew that soon the congregation would be ready to give her a shouting welcome. The way that chorus built up the spirit, it was worth the money—even if the director had asked for a salary Laura never dreamed any church would pay a gospel musicianer. But the tambourines collected it all back, and more sometimes, in a single night.

"Back to the fold,
How safe, how warm I feel!
Back to the fold,
His love alone is real!"

Essie came in and paused at the foot of the iron stairs to drink in the music. "Sounds so good this evening."

"Long as I don't hear Birdie Lee croaking," said Laura. "I believe I'm gonna have to get rid of that old woman."

"Why, the way she hits them drums, the congregation loves her."

"That's just it. I want them to love me—and you—without Birdie's competition. Besides, she just naturally grates on my nerves."

Following Essie by a kiss or two in the hall came Marietta and C.J., bounding lightly into the room.

"Mama, we're going upstairs."

"You and C.J. both should've been up there making music at eight o'clock like the others." Laura was cross tonight.

"It's my fault, Aunt Laura," apologized Marietta. "C.J. came up to Mount Vernon to spend the afternoon with us, and I made a cake that was late getting out of the oven."

"But it was good—ummm-mmm-m!" said C.J.

"Cooking for him already, and you're not married yet. Women are fools," said Laura, looking around for her purse.

"We will be married in the spring, soon's I graduate from high school. Come on, C.J." Marietta pulled him and his guitar toward the stairs.

"He's a nice boy, Laura, and I'm so glad for my child," said Essie.

"I'm glad you got Marietta in the country. Harlem's a den o' sin," growled Laura, rummaging in her pocketbook.

"But don't you reckon our church has made it a little better? Still, I hear some peoples is taking this Temple for a numbers center. Them white gangsters . . ."

"Marty and them 'gangsters,' as you call 'em, squared the violations on this church. It's still a firetrap, you know."

"But we're gradually getting it repaired. And some of the money we're spending like water could . . ."

"If you're talking about my new coat, Essie, you know I always said I was going to have a real *fine* fur some day. You keep on wearing your old rags if you want to, with that same old Lenox Avenue knife of yours in that ragged pocket. What are you protecting?"

Essie laughed, "Nothing. You sure got yourself a pretty beaded purse. But why you dumping everything out on the table?"

"I'm looking for something," said Laura, as she turned the contents of her pocketbook inside out. "I thought I had some of the apple of evil in here—money. You know, I always try to carry a few greenbacks with me. But you, you put all your money except what you live on, back into this church, like a fool. At least, I finally got you to buy yourself a new white velvet robe for the pulpit—up there looking like a scrubwoman, and you the chief saint! Just being robed in goodness, you know, is not enough for the type of folks we attract. They like color, glitter, something to look at along with these fine rhythms we're putting down. I told you that Ed Sullivan mentioned our Tambourine Chorus in his column, didn't I? This church is headed for big money, girl. We're doing all right."

"I ain't for so much publicity," said Essie.

Laura was carefully putting comb, mirror, lipstick, powder, kerchiefs, and odds and ends, one by one, back in her purse as the frown on her face deepened.

"Go on, Essie, get upstairs there and make your presence known, before we start an argument. Anyhow, I want to be the *last* to enter tonight. Sister Mattie, come here!"

Essie got to her knees in one corner and prayed briefly before she panted up the narrow stairs, and the Mistress of the Robes came in to see what Laura wanted.

"Sister Mattie, go up and tell Brother Buddy to come down here a minute—*now!* Suppose you set in with the chorus and sing a little. I want to speak to him *private*."

30

RASCAL OF GOD

Alone, Laura looked at herself in the mirror, carefully in-specting the flow of her scarlet robe before she flung the golden stole about her neck. Upstairs she heard the congregation shouting and clapping and she knew that Essie must have walked onto the rostrum. Suddenly there was a bitter taste in Laura's mouth and a swimming in her head.

I wish Essie would get holy enough or lazy enough or some-thing to quit my Temple, thought Laura, but she won't. The stronger Essie gets in faith, the louder that woman sings and the stouter she sits on the rostrum—and folks just love Essie for *just sitting*. All they have to do is see her up there, and they feel happy. But look at the money I would make without her—and I wouldn't have to split it with no woman, just Buddy. Sometimes, though, I believe Buddy would cheat even me—in fact, I know it. Buddy and Essie! One's *too* honest, and the other one ain't honest enough. Jesus, I got two crosses to bear, and both of 'em's galling my back.

Laura loosened the golden strip of velvet about her neck and softened its folds as a frame for her face. Then she heard his footsteps.

"What wantest thou, Sister Laura?" Buddy mocked, head down, eyes teasing as he came in.

Laura wheeled accusingly, and there were no preliminaries. "Did you take that hundred-dollar bill out of my purse?"

"I *sure* did," smiled Buddy.

"The dough you're getting from this church is not enough?"

"It *sure* ain't," grinned Buddy.

"You're not satisfied?"

"No," smiled Buddy.

It was the sight of his big nonchalant teasing lips with the white teeth between them that infuriated Laura. "So you're planning to spend some more of my dough on that bitch, heh?"

"Watch your language, sister! What bitch?"

"You think I don't know? I mean that cheap little model you've been riding around in that convertible I gave you."

"She's no cheap little model—she can sing. She's got a contract at the Vanguard, moving on up to the Blue Angel. Next thing you know she'll be in the Copa. Marty's underwriting her."

"Somebody'll be *undertaking* her if she don't stay out of that car I bought you. She'll be singing in the Devil's Graveyard with an everlasting contract."

"Ha-ha! Says you!"

"Says I, baby. Brazen as she is with you, it's a wonder it ain't all written up in *Jet*. It will be next week, I expect. *Lorna*—why, even her name sounds like my name!"

"She don't look like you, baby."

"No?"

"Don't kid yourself. I'm a young man, Laura. You're old enough to be my mama."

Laura stood for a moment in silence. Upstairs the choir was singing:

*"God gave the people the rainbow sign—
No more water, but fire next time . . ."*

"Buddy, you don't have to say things to hurt me," Laura said. "I just wondered who took my money, that's all."

"You knew who took your money," Buddy said. "I can have it, can't I?"

"Yes, Buddy, I guess you can have anything I got," she answered quietly. "But now my pocketbook's empty after you made your raid—so I might as well leave it downstairs here. I believe I'll stash it in Essie's old coat pocket."

Laura went toward the hook on the wall where Essie had hung her heavy black coat, and into Essie's pocket she put the beaded purse. For a moment her hand lingered in the pocket there. As she turned to Buddy, the long sleeves of her velvet robe covered both her hands like drooping wings.

"Maybe you can tell me," Laura said, "why it looks like, no matter what a woman does, a man can't never seem to act right? You try to treat a man nice, and looks like he has to turn around and drop the boom on you. Ain't a woman suppose to be nothing but dirt under a man's feet?"

"Just about all, in my opinion," said Buddy. "You feel so good under my feet."

"You don't try to hide *your* ways, do you?"

"Why try? You can't hide nothing from God, can you? Nor the police. So why worry? The police I can pay off—God you *pray* off."

"And me?" asked Laura.

Suddenly Buddy leaned savagely across the table. "You? I'll slap the hell out of you, if you fool with me! A woman like you is supposed to put out some dough—if you want to keep a guy like me around. I don't mean peanuts. Believe me, baby, now that you've got me, *you're gonna keep me*. I ain't gonna give you up. Besides, I'm a partner in this deal—from the Holy Water and the Lucky Texts to the tambourines. You told me, I'm a saint also. What did I go to all that trouble of getting converted for? Since I been functioning in this church, look how many more young girl members you got—just on account of me and my presence. Two beat-up old women saints like you and Essie maybe can pull in those wrecks out of the gutter like Crow-For-Day and Birdie Lee—but me, I bring in the young girls. There's something about me, Laura, that the chicks go for." He looked at her a long time, then smiled. "You admit I'm a m-a-n—*man*, don't you, kid?"

"God gave the people the rainbow sign—
No more water, but fire next time . . ."

Playful again, Buddy from behind put an arm around Laura's neck, pulled her head backward toward him, tall, and kissed her from above, "Hummm-mm-m!"

Laura suddenly thrust her tongue between his teeth. "There *is* . . . something about you, Buddy—doggone it!"

"I know, baby—so the women tell me. There's something about you, too, Laura, now that you're close. . . ."

Suddenly Laura cried, "You sweet rascal of God!"

She turned and, as she found herself in his arms, she let his lips find hers. Swiftly the wide sleeves of her scarlet robe swept upward like velvet wings and suddenly her right hand descended between his shoulder blades—and something in that hand went deeper into Buddy's body than the thrust of her tongue in his warm moist mouth.

Hurrying through the open door at that moment came Sister Birdie Lee who, at the sight of the lovers, paused politely on the threshold before crossing the room. "I'm sorry, you-all, but my kidneys is bad."

Rushing, Birdie cut across the basement toward the sign that said TOILET as Laura stepped back. Suddenly, before Birdie got where she was going, Buddy fell straight forward at Laura's feet and the startled Birdie saw him sprawled face downward on the floor with the blade of a gleaming white switchblade knife stuck in his back. The spreading ooze of blood stained his jacket.

"Oh!" said Birdie Lee. "Lemme get to the bathroom."

Birdie rushed in and closed the door. Laura stood where she was over Buddy's body, but her eyes followed the woman. "You had better not come out—you hear me, Birdie Lee? Unless you are struck dumb. Speechless! I say, struck dumb!" When Birdie pulled the chain and emerged, Laura repeated, "Did you hear what I said?"

"Yes, Sister Laura," the little black woman trembled, "I heard."

"You'd better be speechless, Birdie! If you so much as open your mouth anywhere to anybody, with my own hands I'll . . ."

As the scarlet sleeves fell back from her brown arms, Laura's fists went up into the air and their fingers opened like two frightening claws. The words choked in her throat. When she got her voice back, Laura shooed the petrified Birdie to the door. "Get back upstairs to your drums, you evil hussy! Give me a *big* drum roll when I make my entrance to the pulpit. You hear me—a *big* drum roll!"

Birdie tumbled up the stairs. From the pocket of Essie's coat Laura took her purse, looked down at Buddy motionless on the floor, then ascended to the altar where the music swirled.

31

EVERLASTING ARM

"Oh, this world is just my dressing room,
But now, at last, dear Lord, I'm coming home.
Down in the mire too long my feet have trod.
Now, at last, I'll make my home in God."

Walking in rhythm out from the wings, her scarlet robes sway-ing, Laura advanced toward the congregation as a thousand hands clapped in time to the music, the tambourines trilled, the drums rolled, and the trumpet gleamed, its notes round and full.

"Thank God!" said Laura. "Thank Him for His son, for the Holy Ghost, for Sister Essie, for the Tambourine Chorus, the Gloriettas, and for this great church here tonight. Also for this Holy Water, precious fluid from the Jordan, imported just for you. Blessed water to purify your home, one dollar a bottle, friends, just one dollar! While I sing, ushers, pass amongst the people with these bottles. If they run low, there's more here beside me on the rostrum. While Sister Essie goes into the wings for meditation, pass amongst the people with the water."

Essie, who never stayed on the platform for this performance, rose, bowed her head, and walked off while Laura sang:

> "I'm going to lay down my soul
> At the foot of the cross,
> Yes, and tell my Jesus
> Just what sin has cost . . ."

The Tambourine Choir joined with her in the singing, so loud and strong that no one heard the startled scream that suddenly echoed from the room below the stage.

"Now, comes the time for testimonials," said Laura, "for one and all to declare his determination. And I ask you with a song:

> "Who will be a witness for my Lord?
> For my Lord? For my Lord?
> Who will be a witness for my Lord
> On the day of jubilee?"

It had not occurred to Laura that a cracked old voice would sing out behind her without missing a beat on the drums:

> "I will be a witness for my Lord!
> For my Lord! Yes, for my Lord!
> I will be a witness for my Lord
> On the day of jubilee!"

And at that moment the spotlight of the spirit fell on Birdie Lee who took the song away from the star. Birdie Lee could sing louder than Laura.

This just is *not* my night, Laura thought, wheeling to stare at the little old drummer in the corner above the chorus. "Well, since Birdie Lee seems to want to take over," she said to Marietta seated in the front row of the singers, "you go downstairs and tell your mother she can return from her meditations and be a witness, too."

Birdie Lee ceased her drumming and stood up defiantly to testify. Laura, thinking fast, took a seat in her big red chair behind the rostrum and said "Amen!" Suddenly, a serpent with a diamond in its head whispered to Laura as Birdie Lee talked.

"I want to tell you-all what it means to be a witness, a witness for God, and a witness for men and women, too," cried Birdie. "I were in a trial once, a court trial, and I lied. I let an innocent man go to jail for a crime he didn't do, to protect some old Negro I thought I loved. Another man, innocent as a lamb, served time. But that old Negro I lied for lived to beat up, and cut up and shoot up two or three more people. In fact, that man did not appreciate what I did for him by not telling. Fact is, he lived to kick my—excuse me, I meant to say, to mistreat me, too. That man were so mean he wouldn't let me do a damn, excuse me, I mean not a blessed thing. I'm just excited tonight, folks. But I tries always to keep bad words out of my mouth, now that I'm a Christian woman. What I'm trying to say to everybody this evening is, that when the time comes, in God's name, I got a determination, and my determination is *I'm gonna testify!*" And her speech blended into song, the old song that Birdie liked to sing as she picked up her drumsticks and started to drum.

"I'm gonna testify!
Yes, I'm gonna testify!
I'm gonna testify till the day I die—
Gonna tell the truth
For the truth don't lie.
Folks, I'm gonna testify!"

She fixed her gaze on Laura and sent her voice darting down from her corner across the rostrum and out to the people.

"I did not know such strength I'd find.
Thank God A-Mighty, I'm a gospel lion!
Things I've seen, I cannot keep.
Thank God A-Mighty, God does not sleep!
I'm gonna testify! Yes, testify—
Tell the truth—For the truth don't lie.
Yes, I'm gonna testify!"

"Aunt Laura! Laura! Aunt Laura!" It was Marietta's voice calling shrill and frightened from the wings.

Laura rose and addressed the church. "Excuse me, saints, let me go see what little Sister Marietta wants so urgent. She's calling. Till I resume my seat on the rostrum, we'll turn the services over to our beloved deacon known in love to all of us as Brother Crow-For-Day. Deacon, come forward, and raise a song."

"Leaning, leaning . . .
Leaning, leaning,
On the everlasting arm . . ."

As the massed chorus raised its hardy voices behind her, Laura walked in her scarlet robe with long sleeves flowing toward the steps that led below.

If the Tambourine Chorus had not been singing so lustily behind Crow-For-Day, those on the rostrum might have heard a piercing wail of pretended anguish beneath the stage, and Laura's voice crying, "Essie, you've killed Buddy! Essie, you done killed Buddy! Oh-ooo-oo-o! I know you never did like him, now you've killed him! You killed my Buddy!"

32

JUDAS IN SCARLET

Laura groveled on the basement floor, careful never to touch Buddy's blood, nor put her hands near the body. "Buddy! Buddy, baby, darling! What she done to you? What's Essie done to you?"

Sensing something wrong, from her place in the chorus, Sister Mattie Morningside came bustling down the iron steps in the room beneath the stage. What she saw caused her to stop in her tracks and shake like jelly on a plate.

"Police! Sister Mattie, get the police," screamed Laura. "Look what Essie Johnson's done done to Buddy Lomax."

"Jesus, help us, Jesus!" Sister Mattie moaned on her way to the street in search of the Law.

When the three were alone, Laura turned on the silent Essie

who stood as if in a trance with Marietta weeping beside her. "So this is the way you even scores, heh, Essie? It's *your* knife stuck in his back!"

"Laura, you know I didn't do it."

"There's blood on your robe."

"When I bent over him to see if I could help him, I got blood all on me."

"Why didn't you help Buddy when he was living? No, you wouldn't do that! You wouldn't help us then. You're too good, too sanctified. But he was smart. Buddy had ideas, the Holy Water, them Lucky Texts, ideas for making you and me both rich and happy, but you hated him! So holy, you! Now you've up and committed murder! How could you do this to me, Essie? How could you do it?"

"You know I didn't, Laura."

"Mama wouldn't do anything like that," cried Marietta. "She couldn't! You know she couldn't."

"That's what you think, Little Miss Holier-Than-Thou. I've known your mother longer than you have, and she's always carried a knife."

"Don't worry, honey," said Essie gently to her daughter, "God will straighten this out."

Two policemen, one white and one colored, rushed in followed by the panting Sister Morningside and Laura's wizened little chauffeur. The scarlet sleeves of Sister Laura's robe waved wildly toward Buddy, then toward Essie.

"Look, officers! Her knife in his back and nobody down here but her. Blood on her robe! Essie Johnson killed Buddy. Brother Buddy! Oh-ooo-oo-o! and he just got converted last month!"

Laura buried her head on Sister Mattie Morningside's ample bosom and sobbed for the benefit of the Law.

"Don't nobody touch the body," said the white officer. "We'll send for the coroner." To the colored officer he said, "Put that woman in the squad car." The woman his thumb indicated was Essie.

Upstairs the church was singing "Get on Board, Little Children" while tambourines shook ecstatically.

33

WATCH WITH ME

By and by, when the morning comes,
Saints and sinners all are gathered home.
I'll tell the story how we overcome,
And I'll understand it better by and by . . .

"If they send me to the electric chair," mused Essie, "I'll understand it better after I get to Beulah. But I don't want to die, nor be put away in the penitentiary for life. I got my child to live for, I got my daughter, and I got my church."

Watch with me one hour
While I go yonder and pray.

Just watch with me one hour
While I go yonder and pray . . .

There were exactly twenty-four bars to her cell and Essie sat behind all twenty-four. She had never been in jail before. It was like being in hell. That night cold sweat popped out on her brow—as she figured sweat must have popped out on the brow of Christ when He was praying in the Garden.

Were you there when they crucified my Lord?
Were you there when they nailed Him to the Cross?
Oh, sometimes it causes me to tremble, tremble!
Were you there when they crucified my Lord?

In the dark of the garden, alone, Jesus, who had said, "Before the cock crow, thou shalt deny me thrice," said also, "Friend, wherefore art thou come?" And Judas kissed Jesus on the cheek and betrayed Him. Peter said, "I do not know the man." And the cock crowed.

I must walk this lonesome valley,
Got to walk it for myself.
Nobody else can walk it for me.
I got to walk it for myself.

The old melodies came back to Essie in a flood of song as she sat alone in her cell.

The blood came tricklin' down
And He never said a mumblin' word.
Not a word, not a word, not a word . . .

They plaited a crown of thorns and they put it on His head.

> *And they pierced Him in the side*
> *And He never said a mumblin' word . . .*

If Jesus could stand what they done to Him, I reckon I can stand what's done to me. Only if I just had my Bible to read! After all, I reckon

> *It's nobody's fault but mine,*
> *If I die and my soul gets lost*
> *It's nobody's fault but mine.*

I should have riz in my wrath and cleaned house, Essie thought staring at the walls—which is what I guess is the matter with me all these years, setting—just setting doing nothing but accepting what comes, receiving the Lord's blessing whilst the eagle foulest His nest, till the sinner gets struck down by somebody else with my own knife in his back. I let Buddy fill the house of God with sin, and vanities of vanities take over, and Laura parade her fur coat and purr in her fine car before them poor people what brought us their hard-earned money for God's work—to which only such a little miteful did go. Religion has got no business being made into a gyp game. Whatever part of God is in anybody *is not to be played with*—and everybody has got a part of God in them.

I let Laura play with God—me, Essie Belle Johnson—when I should have riz in my wrath and cleaned house.

34

ONE OF THE LEAST

The next morning Essie stood with her hands on the bars and looked at Marietta. "Daughter, I did not mean to ever let you see your mama in a place like this."

"But, Mama, I got news, news, good news! They found finger-prints on that knife—just like Aunt Laura's. And, Mama, Birdie Lee, Sister Birdie Lee went to the police and told them last night how some hoodlums had already threatened to kill her. But this morning she girded herself in the strength of the Lord, and got herself a lawyer, and went to the Precinct House and told them that when she ran downstairs to the toilet Sunday night she saw Aunt Laura with her hand at Buddy's back, and that knife was there, too—*in his back.* Then Buddy fell flat on his face in front of her before she could get to the bathroom, and he bled. Birdie Lee swears Aunt Laura killed Buddy herself just before Laura came upstairs for services. And Mama, your lawyer says you'll be out soon, maybe by afternoon, quick as he gets down here with the papers. And Sister Birdie Lee, she's outside in the Reception Room waiting to see you now, but they wouldn't let her in being she's not a relative, unless you say you want to see her. She's brought you a Bible. You'd like to see her, wouldn't you, Mama?"

"Birdie Lee and the Bible *both* your mama wants to see, Marietta."

"Then I'll tell them to let her in. And I'll be back to get you with the lawyer."

When the turnkey brought Birdie Lee down through the aisle of cells she began to shout *Hallelujahs* even before she saw Essie, and *Bless Gods* and *Amens*. She cried as she stood before the cell, "I have brought the Book. But before I give it to you, Essie, I want to read thereout and therefrom and I want you to listen— Matthew 25—for Sister Essie: 'I was an hungered, and ye gave me meat. I was thirsty, and ye gave me drink. I was a stranger, and ye took me in.' In spite of Laura Reed! Sister Essie, the light is the truth, and the truth don't lie. 'Naked, and ye clothed me. I was sick, and ye visited me. I was in prison,' yes, the prison of my sins, 'and ye came unto me.' "

Birdie slapped her hand down on the Bible.

"It's right here in His holy Word, Essie, how you took me out of the gutter of Lenox Avenue, raised me up to the curbstone of redemption, brought me into your gospel band, and let me shake my tambourine to the glory of God and drum my way to jubilation. Sister Essie, you did that for me! Gangsters or no gangsters, Laura or no Laura, it's my determination to testify exactly who stuck that knife in Big-Eyed Buddy's carcass—to take the stand

and tell the truth—for the truth don't lie! And listen to this text through your bars of sorrow, Sister Essie, for it appears as if these words was writ for you—Matthew 25:40—'Verily,' it says here, 'verily I say unto you, inasmuch as ye have done it unto one of the *least* of these'—and I was the least—'ye have done it unto me!' Hallelujah! Oh, if I had just brought my tambourine, I would shake it here in jail to God's glory, to you, Sister Essie, who by your goodness lifted me up out of the muck and mire of Harlem and put my feet on the rock of grace where I, Birdie Lee, can stand and redeem myself of the lies I once told and the souls sent to hell—this time to testify the truth! Praise God, your Honor, Judge Almighty, I'm gonna testify!"

35

AS IN A DREAM

When the jailers brought her lunch, Essie was reading in her Book the verses Birdie had found for her. She saw in her mind's eye Laura who had clothed herself in a scarlet robe and had made her buy a white one, and she remembered white being for purity. And she thought, Laura brought me to God, but I was too slothful to save my friend from sin. I did not try hard enough in God's ways. But I pray now in my heart for Laura.

It seemed almost like a dream, or a scene in a movie, that now a key should turn in the door at the end of the cell block, and the door should open, and clank, and close, and a warden should lead down the aisle a fine frame of a woman with her head down, not looking to the right or the left as she passed, until Essie cried, "Laura!"

There with her hands on the bars, with the bars between them, stood her partner in song. A long pause, then, "Essie, I'm sorry," Laura whispered hoarsely, "sorry as hell for what I did to you—and with your knife, too. The Law knows now that I did it. I confessed. I might as well. That little rat of a Birdie Lee put the finger on me. I never did like Birdie. But I would have told, anyhow. Believe me or not, Essie, I got down on my knees last night and prayed. I couldn't sleep for thinking about you in jail, and Buddy dead. The two people I loved most in my life! And the fault mine! I would have told the police anyhow I did it. Essie, can you find it in your heart to just, maybe, pray for me?"

"You're my friend, Laura. In spite of all, you been my friend. In my heart eternal, I pray for you—and I'll see that you get a lawyer, too."

"A dozen lawyers phoned me already this morning. They think I got money. But I took all the hundred-dollar bills I had stashed away in drawers and car pockets and handkerchief boxes, and places, and put them in the bank early this morning when it opened, in the church's name before the police came to question me. Essie, I'll come before the bar of justice as poor as I was that night when we left out of that tenement and took our stand for the first time to raise a song on Lenox Avenue. My car, the dealers can take back. It's not paid for. I have nothing now, Essie, but Jesus—since He comes free." Laura smiled a wry smile. "Maybe somebody'll buy me a drink."

It was a long cell block and they locked Laura in a cell far down at the end of the corridor, so far away that Laura did not hear Essie sobbing. Essie sobbed as quietly as she could, but it was hard for a big woman like Essie to weep so bitterly without a sound.

36

JUBILATION

"What He's done for me!
What He's done for me!
I never shall forget
What He's done for me!
He took my feet out of the mirey clay.
He set them on a rock to stay . . ."

"I never shall forget," cried Essie, "what He's done for me."

A thousand people in the temple, and a hundred in the chorus behind her sang.

"He put a song in my soul today.
What He's done for me!"

"Done for all of us," cried Essie. "Praise His name! All you who helped to make this church, to raise its walls from the curbstone to this rostrum, helped me to buy the first tambourine I ever had in my hand! Tambourine Temple, I want to tell you what, with His help, we're gonna do. Here on this very corner, I visions me a Rock. Today I seen the contractor. We're gonna turn that big room downstairs into a pretty day nursery where you mothers that goes to work can leave your children. Oh, Rock of Comfort, free from worry! I seen the real estate man. We're gonna buy that old building next door and turn it into a clubhouse where you can meet to have your anniversaries and parties and such. Oh, joyful Rock! That empty vacant lot three doors down, we're gonna turn into an outdoor playground so our teenagers can play basketball in summer and flood it with ice so they can skate in winter. Happy Rock! Oh, friends, so many nice things we're gonna do for this Harlem of ours with His help! And now, folks, another announcement, my earthly aid from this day on, my staff of youth in this church and in this pulpit, is my daughter, Marietta! She's going to study next fall at the Lincoln Hospital to be a nurse so she can help me take care of the sick in this church. While I pray with the sick, Marietta can tend them and relieve their pain. Come forward, daughter."

"Jehovah God!" cried Birdie Lee. "Jehovah God!"

Marietta stepped down shyly from the choir. Essie beamed.

"This is Marietta Johnson. But there's more I want to tell you about her. She won't be Johnson long. She will have a helper or he will have his helper, both will help each other, the son of this temple, our son, C.J., to be my son-in-law."

"Amen!" affirmed the crowd. "God bless them both." Then silence that Marietta might speak.

"It's wonderful to be in love with God," the girl said, "and with this church, with you-all before me, and C.J."

Essie beckoned C.J. forward to join hands with Marietta. "Now, let them praise God together, and all of us praise God with them—Marietta, C.J.—*our children!* Hit your guitar, son! Let my daughter sing."

"Rise and shine
And give God the glory!"

"Shake, tambourines, shake! Help 'em, Crow-For-Day, help 'em! Drum it, Birdie Lee! Drum to the Lord God Jehovah! Drum for the least of His servants, me, Essie Belle Johnson! Halleloo! And, folks—

"If you've got a tambourine,
Shake it to the glory of God!
Glory! Glory! Glory!
Shake it to the glory of God!
Tambourines! Tambourines!
Tambourines to glory!
  Tambourines!
  Tambourines
  To glory!"

Reading Group Companion

———

1. Langston Hughes originally wrote *Tambourines to Glory* as a play. If you were to direct a theatrical production of *Tambourines,* what elements of direction, scenery, and score would you use to dramatize characters and scenes in the narrative?

2. As she is depicted in the beginning of *Tambourines to Glory,* would you describe Laura Reed as *a*moral or *im*moral?

3. Essie Johnson is portrayed as a humble, pious, and earnest woman. Laura Reed, on the other hand, is hedonistic, selfish, and conniving. How effective are Laura and Essie as foils for each other? Is the stark contrast between the two

women effective in elucidating each character? Do these portrayals seem realistic or allegorical?

4. If Essie worships a trinity of the Father, the Son, and the Holy Spirit, what trinity does Laura worship? What are her acts of worship?

5. Discuss how Laura appropriates and uses the language of the gospel to support her secret agenda and to defend her behavior.

6. Despite her deceitful nature, Laura positively affects the spiritual lives of members of her congregation. Does the moral deficiency of the messenger necessarily detract from the message? Explain.

7. Though Essie is portrayed as generally moral and good, she is not without fault and not without blame. What is Essie's sin? Of what is she guilty? Passivity? Idleness?

8. On those occasions when Laura sells bogus holy water to members of the congregation, Essie withdraws from what is going on and meditates. Hughes writes, "Essie's life had been full of long, long, very long pauses" (page 16). What happens when Essie goes into "pause" mode? Do you think her pause is a show of commendable patience and long suffering? Or is it evidence of passivity and listlessness? How can a "pause" mode be a psychological defense mechanism?

9. Does Laura's humor and wit ever soften the harshness of her bad deeds? Did you find Laura to be likable despite her evildoing?

10. How does the frequent incorporation of gospel lyrics in *Tambourines to Glory* shape or affect the narrative?

11. In the opening of *Tambourines to Glory,* the women exchange stories about their mothers. Neither woman mentions a father, nor does Essie ever reference her daughter Marietta's father. What significance does the omission of fathers have for the story?

12. Marty is a puppet master of sorts. He is a powerful and well-connected criminal who pulls strings, coerces, and manipulates from behind the scenes—and he is white. What is the effect of having Marty never actually appear in the story? What does Hughes's second- and thirdhand depiction of Marty—the most significant white character in the story— suggest about the role and function of whites in this largely segregated black community? How are white people generally depicted in (or excluded from) *Tambourines to Glory*?

13. How does Buddy transform Laura? Accordingly, how does the introduction of Buddy into the text change the course and tone of the story?

14. In what ways does Hughes romanticize and glamorize black life in Harlem? In what ways is he critical of it?

About the Author

LANGSTON HUGHES is one of our most acclaimed and revered writers and the leading figure of the Harlem Renaissance. Over his forty-year career he worked as a novelist, poet, playwright, newspaper columnist, and children's book author, in addition to his role as editor for numerous anthologies and short story collections. He died in 1967, in Harlem.